# FRIENDS OF D. STROBOS

SEMYON WHITE

Ordering Information:

Prime Seven Media
518 Landmann St.
Tomah City, WI 54660

Printed in the United States of America

"We have our gods, erected our monuments
and houses of worship. We study our
canons of catechism, yet live by the
movement and grace of the sun."

S WHITE

# Table of Contents

*I am writing in response to your initial email detailing my orders. My position in forensics makes it commonplace for me to examine and evaluate many suspects. I've often been called upon to confirm their allegiances, even investigate the premises of improbable testimony, so I understood why you chose me for the assignment. The suspect in your inquiries, however, I initially took to be a hoax. A chimera, a razor-sharp feature of an awful and enabling delusion.*

*Only the repetition of the name 'Strobos' and various confirmed details of his appearance and personal effects prompted me to search further to confirm story events with relevant news sources. A police report surfaced about a Donny Strobos who matches the description of the suspect.*

*I have compiled several first hand accounts of witnesses and accusers indicating a sole perpetrator. They illustrate his methods, practices, and even motivations to some extent.*

*I don't know if all of their content will be helpful as each of these seemingly rational persons has made claims to have experienced the magical or the impossible.*

*They speak of awful acts of inhuman violence, yet some have described a humane nature in the suspect.*

*We have been fortunate with eyewitness accounts from people who have survived an encounter with the suspect or one of his unstable accomplices. These encounters often result in brief psychological codependence or an entanglement. This entanglement is most serious when a suspect exhibits any degree of purposeful manipulation or apparent control of an anomaly.*

*In an era where much of what once appeared to be magical or mysterious has been realized through science, the magical and mysterious have become more readily accepted as the manifestations of unknown science or technology, thereby increasingly plausible to the public. In the many cases*

*I've encountered involving survivors of an entanglement, they are very forthcoming, and even compelled to relate their accounts because of the impact the alleged entanglements have had on their perceptions and systems of belief. I'm certain the entangled have encountered something inexplicable, something unknown and they are all changed by it.*

*Some of their testimonies are from statements in video clips made after their arrests, others are compiled narratives from recorded sessions of psychoanalysis at our facilities. Included are stories based on statements and allegations from interviews with the entangled I've conducted personally.*

*I have included transcripts which illustrate the suspect's abilities for study and evaluation of weaponized tech.*

Others serve as studies into his allegiances and personal motivational factors.

To make sense of the suspect's actions may aid in the generation of behavioral patterns which in turn become the basis for predictive courses of investigation and apprehension, if possible.

I will be in touch with further developments on the entangled associates of this suspect, these "Friends of D. Strobos," so to speak. In collecting data, I have made attempts at drawing conclusions and have abandoned just as many.

SSgt. F. Chandrastakar
Division of Forensic Studies
2057.11.05

# 1

# BLACK CAR SERVICE

## 2001

The sky had been the insane pink which only occurred with any regularity in the fall. Sunset was when vampires dreamed. It was the toss and turn time for the Terrible, fraught with idealized kills, anxious images of dangerous wooden objects, and recurrent scenarios of flight from volcanic dawns of molten sunlight destroying everything it touched. I know this because Strobos told me his dreams.

One hot night in the summer, he'd walked into the dispatcher's office with a clipping from the classified ads. We shook hands, his was ice cold. A chill ran up my elbow and made the hair on the back of my neck bristle. We needed drivers for the night shift. Everyone who came in looked like the worst of all possible losers and if they didn't, I worried.

Pale and gaunt, dark glasses, cold as ice; another drug addict, I thought but he was fluent in English which made him cream of the crop. If a normal, hardworking human being drove a car for a living these days, he was usually from South America, Africa or the Middle East. All the native English speakers who applied were ex-cons, drug addicts, psychos or horrible life long fuckups. The squeaky clean daylight world simply had no room for them, neither did the more reputable medallion taxi agencies with their exams, drug tests, and criminal history checks.

A black car service was different. All we required of our employees were three or four functioning limbs and at least one operable eye. A driver's license was also a good thing but I can't say I haven't let it slide on occasion as long as I believed the driver had passed the road test at some point in life.

Our drivers couldn't legitimately pick up fares on the street like the yellow medallion cars but it was done nevertheless where the long arm of the law fell a little short. Black cars seemed to maneuver better in gray areas.

Dionysis Strobos showed me an international license with no photo. He'd said his new one was in the mail. I had heard that one before and it didn't stop me from putting him in a black car.

I considered him briefly upon handing over the keys. He looked late-twenties or mid- thirties, had longish dark hair pulled sloppily away from his face with a rubber band that sat on the back of his head. Over a black hooded sweatshirt, he wore an old dark gray pinstriped three piece. It was a bit much for August. Maybe he'd worn the suit to impress me. It probably would have, if it had ever been pressed. I told him he could start right away.

The next evening, he returned with a big trash bag over his shoulder looking very much like an overgrown runaway. I guessed the bag was stuff for his locker; an old sweater or two, a raincoat, maybe his favorite coffee mug - nothing unusual. It was months before I found out what was in that bag.

I expected the night drivers around 11:30 PM, Strobos would appear around ten or so and sit at the lunch table in the garage scanning the personals or reading news. He always wore the same suit or a variation of the three pieces every night. When ready for work, he would drive out and come back just before sunrise. If a driver made his quota early, who was I to care if he wanted to call it a night? As long as he was back at the garage and available if I needed him, it was fine.

One evening, I came in early. The second shift's dispatcher, Jackie French, was on his dinner break somewhere and none of his day drivers were back yet. It was the only real quiet time, the time between shifts.

There were some new floor mats in the loft upstairs. I wanted to have them down in the office to give out to each man when his shift began. If anyone was going to break in the new mats, it would be my crew.

Climbing down, carrying the second big cardboard box, I thought I saw Strobos getting out of the trunk of a big old Lincoln up on cinderblocks in the back of the garage. Later, when he sat at his usual spot reading personals and drinking what he told us was tomato soup, I went back to look in the Lincoln's trunk.

The Lincoln was an older Limo from the late sixties. The company's owner kept it because he was certain it would be valuable when he finished collecting enough of the parts to restore it. I think its value had something to do with the Kennedy Assassination and the so-called *suicide doors*.

Now it just sat there, no engine, no wheels or doors, up on the blocks, rusting into oblivion. I pulled the stiff trunk release and walked back to raise the heavy chrome lined black steel.

There was dirt, a torn trash bag and a little cloth drawstring case. I squeezed it in my hand and felt hard cylindrical parts that quickened my pulse. I pulled it open and some very old tarnished brass pieces came out. It looked like what was left of an old alto sax, not the gun I'd envisioned seconds earlier.

I looked at the small parts in my hand and back to the ancient limo. A guy in a vintage suit liked old things. Nothing unusual about that at all. I guessed Strobos must have been admiring the old heap, it was after all supposed to be a classic. Lots of the new guys looked at it. It didn't explain why he was getting cozy in the trunk, but it seemed harmless.

A week later, I found Ronnie Kolodny waiting in the dispatcher's office, pacing back and forth. Kolodny was a short and stocky Ukrainian fifty-something. He had been a sailor and always wore a black watch cap over his cropped silver hair regardless of season. He was day shift, one of Jackie French's guys. Kolodny was a drinker but not nearly enough for him to qualify amongst the ranks of my fuck-ups on nights. He grabbed my forearm and took me out behind the garage where his car was parked. I lit a cigarette and took a big drag.

"I have something to show you," he mumbled leading me to it.

"Couldn't you just tell me?" I hated surprises. Back in '98 someone had given birth in one of our cars and a week later the placenta showed up under the fold down arm rest in the middle of the rear bench.

"Blood," Kolodny whispered coarsely, "Much blood."

I looked at the blood splattered on the back seat and on the floor. Most of it had dried. "There go the new floor mats," I said. Blood was nothing new. Blood, vomit, piss, used condoms; they all had their place in the night so it didn't bother me any more than the evening news.

Then there had been a couple of high profile killings last fall. The victims were young women found in nearby Long Island City.

The papers had run bold capitals spelling *BEHEADED* on the front page. The women were identified by the tattoos they had on their lower backs which were so popular for a while. I remembered thinking that those tattoos had finally been good for something other than giving a guy a little distraction as he fornicated.

I blew smoke over Kolodny and tried to sound professional enough to settle the dayshifter's concerns.

"You pick up anyone hurt?" I asked stupidly.

"Nobody hurt. This is old blood. Blood from the night. Customers complain."

"I guess. Well, get it cleaned up. Put in a petty cash slip, take it to the car wash."

"No, we wait. I called police," Kolodny said, getting loud.

"Shit." The last thing I needed were the authorities poking their noses around my crew of dead beat dads, dope fiends, bail jumpers and illegals.

"Jackie told me to call," he said. Jackie French, the morning dispatcher, was an older black guy, ex-Marine, by the book, eggs and coffee early riser. I glanced at the number on the plate. It was the car Strobos drove. I was sure French wasn't waiting around for the police and would be happy to leave the mess for me.

"Okay, Ronny. I'll take it from here." I took a last deep drag and flicked the butt against the wall and it burst away in an orange plume of hot particles.

"I'm sorry. It's too much blood," he said, nodding his head as he walked back inside.

As the season changed and it was darker earlier and stayed darker longer. D. Strobos would appear just after dusk, hours before I came in. There were always a few drivers with no lives, friends or anything to do all day. They might come in early, shoot the shit, play cards, share pizzas, whatever. He'd sit at the lunch tables for an hour or more searching through newspapers and staring into a small tablet.

Sometimes he'd wander around outside listening to music on headphones, sipping his soup. For a younger guy, he was a real loner, maybe even what some might call eccentric. No wonder Kolodny left the car out back. He didn't want to sit and wait for me with a quiet weirdo who had blood in his car.

I found D. Strobos in his usual spot reading a paper.

"How's it going?" I pulled up a seat alongside. He bobbed his head in positive satisfaction.

"Anything unusual happen on last night's shift?" I asked, casually as possible, looking around the room meaninglessly.

"No."

He must've know his car wasn't in the garage waiting for him, but it wasn't time for him to drive yet anyway. I looked at his paper. He was scanning the old style personals column.

"Looking for a lady?" I'd asked, smirking.

"I'm looking for eternal love," he stated flatly.

"That's a tall order for the *Village Voice*." Just then the police walked in and ambled over to dispatcher's office. I followed. "Well, my night's getting interesting it seems," I said in stride. Strobos put on his shades and went over to the lockers.

I had told the police the driver picked up a fare uptown heading for the emergency room, a stabbing. In all the excitement, he forgot to get it cleaned up afterwards. I also told them the driver in question wasn't in yet, which was only half true. Strobos's shift hadn't begun. They took samples and left business cards.

Later that week a detective called. My story had checked out, even led to an unrelated arrest. A black car had dropped a stabbing victim and his mother off at Mount Sinai Hospital around 3AM. I knew my business. There was always a stabbing uptown. When you had no insurance you called a black car service if you didn't want to bleed out and kick it on the street.

Every evening since, I had watched Strobos sitting there lifelessly, listlessly scanning the papers and sipping his soup before his shift. He looked like a lonely guy coming off a bad breakup, maybe, or a bad divorce like my own. He seemed harmless and shy. Perhaps reticent was a better word than shy.

Maybe some freak bled half to death in his car that night and hadn't said a word. Anything was possible on the night shift. Years ago, I'd picked up a gunshot victim. The man had held his coat closed tightly but it was a cold January evening so it wasn't unusual. He'd just sat in the back seat bleeding and looking out the windows at the last lights of Christmas. I let him out at Penn Station where he took a few steps and collapsed. I drove away. It was none of my business.

One day, Kolodny hadn't shown up for his shift. Two nights had passed before I found out about it. He had just disappeared. That sort of thing happened from time to time.

Loan sharks, deportation, outstanding warrants, bad habits; these things had a way of catching up with a man and he'd leave an opening somewhere which would fill up and be forgotten as well. I thought nothing of it. He wasn't on my shift anyway.

This February was colder than ever. There was a two inch blanket of snow over a week's worth of frozen-over crushed slush and black oil-streaked ice. The crunch-tinkle of the chained tires in the garage as cars came in before dawn was as comforting as the orange hot glow of the space heater under my desk. I wanted to go home and curl up on my sofa under a blanket in front of the TV with a hot mug of scotch, honey and lemon.

The phones were quiet. Everyone was on hold waiting for an available car. Suddenly, I saw Strobos appear in the back of the garage.

He was looking up at the high narrow window over the lockers. He didn't wear a winter coat, only his hoodie and the old three piece. I walked over to him. It had been weeks since we actually spoke but that wasn't unusual. He held a gold pocket watch, its ornate cover open as he wound one of the tiny stems.

"That's quite a timepiece. You mind if I look at it?" He held it out to me. It was attached to his vest on a watch fob that seemed to be a foot or so of braided blonde hair. The hair freaked me out a bit; my hands trembled.

"Cold as hell in here," I said. The braid was frayed and fuzzy, really old-looking which calmed me down a little.

"Cold as Hell," he echoed, making me hear the capital H.

The watch was a nice one, an antique; the kind with a little window which showed a rising sun or rising moon depending on the time of day. I passed it back to him.

"An antique?" I asked, looking at the braided fob as he pocketed the watch.

"Very much so."

"The gold is so dark and smooth. You're into antiques? I saw you looking at the old Lincoln. It's an antique."

"Yes."

"I like the car too. It's the owner's but he doesn't mind us looking at it. Feel free to check it out."

Another car came in. It was Orlando Rojas. I could hear his loud Salsa even with his windows closed. I went over to his car, he always had a complaint so I knew he'd talk. I listened to him tell me about this or that drunken son-of-a-bitch he encountered during the night as I watched D. Strobos disappear behind the old Lincoln.

Back at home, my couch was comfortable. It had to be because I didn't own a bed. I was covered and warm, a little tipsy, watching young black girls shake their asses on MTV. I laughed out loud, finally drunk, so I could pass out. Why should I give a shit if some sad weirdo wanted to sleep in the dirty old trunk of an old car at the garage? I only worked there, and I knew I'd slept one off from time to time up in the loft. Rent was a fortune in New York City and quite the burden on a single guy. I could barely afford my little two room studio. Maybe he was saving his money up. That would explain his limited wardrobe too. None of that made him a psycho killer. I slept dreamlessly.

A week or so later, sometime after five AM, I stepped out for a smoke behind the garage in the twilight. Melting snow had become fog. On the back street there was a car, one of ours. I lit up and walked towards it. I could hear some anxious noises, then D. Strobos came out and walked back to the trunk. It seemed someone was in it, kicking and banging. He opened the trunk with the key. There was an inexplicably fast flash of metal. He pushed a small limp feminine hand back inside and slammed the trunk shut. Then he turned to me, apparently knowing I'd been there all along.

Strobos stood looking at me look at him. It felt like one of those instants when you came across a wild animal in the woods and it had noticed you at the same moment. It was the grounded, inert stillness that possessed both man and beast in moments of mortal uncertainty. I took another drag from my cigarette, gave him a slight nod then dropped the butt, watched it fall and slowly smeared it out in the cold dampness with my foot. When I looked up again it was just in time to see him close his door and pull away.

I don't know to this day why I had agreed to help him when I did. I guess we were all fuck-ups on the night shift, I was no different.

It had been another night in darkest February past, a wild and windy star-strewn night in Westchester. The TV was on but it had been long ago when a station would actually end its broadcast day sometime after 1AM and a bleak little tone would whine off into the night.

She had turned the set off after coming home to find me passed out on our bed in front of it. That sudden quiet had woken me. I'll never forget the feeling of my arms trembling as I held the pillow over my wife's head, pressing and pressing, hoping to break her fucking neck because she wouldn't suffocate soon enough and kept clawing at my arms and face. The wind howled and howled, pulling at my roof tiles, rattling the storm gutters in the dire silence. When she finally gave in, I rolled off her and sat to catch my own breath. Then I panicked and shook her and shook her, kissed her face and rubbed her upper arms and chest. She had still been warm. I found her weak pulse. I went down to the kitchen and poured myself a drink, a really big one.

I was hungover, bloodied and reeked of booze when the police dragged me away that morning. The order of protection, a prison stint, cheap motels and divorce had followed.

My former employer was a women's sports apparel manufacturer. When my wife's attorney had informed them of some of my divorce's details, I lost my position. The last laugh was on her because I never found work in the same industry despite my experience and couldn't afford to pay a substantial alimony. My wife ended up selling the house and moving back in with her family.

For nearly a decade afterwards, I'd wished every night that I had actually killed her. I'd be at a red light in a herd of traffic in the middle of a rain, wipers beating big drops, or sitting in a cheap shithole chasing cockroaches with a cigarette, thinking I should have killed the bitch.

Maybe seeing that little hand with the painted nails being shoved back into the trunk satisfied something wicked in me, some form of vicarious wish fulfillment. Rationalizations were easy but they never covered everything. You couldn't rationalize for everything you feel in life especially the things which couldn't easily be put into words.

I was no stranger to trouble with women, I didn't really believe any man was. If D. Strobos did turn out to be a real lady killer, I had hoped remotely that he had or would kill mine. Besides, I wasn't a policeman.

Detecting or preventing crime wasn't any of my business. Further, if he was a crazy serial killer targeting women, he wasn't out to kill me and I didn't have a daughter or sister out there in harm's way. Fuck everybody else.

Not my problem. He wasn't hacking up the fares either, as far as I could tell.

But the nightmares began, which up until recently, I had believed were only for little children. I saw blood pouring out of black cars, D. Strobos; a black shadow as insubstantial as movement in the clouds, rooms pilled high with clipped braids and ringed fingers.

The nightmares were getting in the way of sleep and that propelled me to investigate further, find something tangible. I had checked his car a couple of times after the trunk incident and found nothing initially, so I had to let it go. Disbelief had played a part. What I witnessed behind the garage had been quick, unreal and had no aftermath.

The police hadn't returned. D. Strobos never freaked out when he saw me later that night or the next.

There was one small item in his trunk that escaped detection on my fast and furtive inspections; the curved spike heal of a red leather pump. I had taken it home. I looked at it in my ashtray guiltily every evening on my way out the door to work. Found elsewhere in the car, it would be meaningless. In the trunk it was troubling.

One of the day guys had the newspaper clippings of those beheaded women and their tailbone tattoos taped up on his locker. There were now five or six of them. It seemed the killer hadn't stopped, just stopped making headlines. Only day shift people could be entertained with the morbid. Senseless, grizzly killings only added up to humorous chit chat at the water cooler. Too many night workers in this city have lived through enough bad shit to find those news items funny.

Strobos was in the dispatcher's office with Jackie French. French had every old street atlas spread out on the desk and floor. Very excited, he turned to where I lurked in the doorway.

"It seems your boy here knows every goddamn street in the five boroughs," he said, standing up over the mess of maps.

"Is that so?" I asked without much enthusiasm. Strobos grinned at me wryly.

"I've just walked around a lot," Strobos told us.

"I never met a driver who knew more about Brooklyn than I did," French said, laughing as he looked up at the clock and started to clear away the maps. I walked out with Strobos to give French some space as he got ready to go home. He always called his old lady just before departing and I couldn't stand to listen to him cooing at her over the phone.

"Mr. French told me there had been two night shifts but you took them both on, combined the two," Strobos said emphasizing his approval.

"Not exactly," I said.

"But there is only *one* night shift."

"It just made it easier for you guys, gave you more flexibility in when you worked. Let you play your nights by ear. None of us ever liked words like punctuality," I explained.

"But it's more than that isn't it, if you don't mind my saying. You love the *nighttime*, the sense of wild potential that falls over the city," he said quietly, gauging my reaction.

"Where are you going with this?"

"I know you are curious about something and I am curious as well Mr. Grislundt," he said, looking directly into my eyes.

"Whatever you do is your business. I extend that courtesy to all the guys and I expect the same. Just bring us the cash at the end of the night and try to keep the car in one piece. That's all I ask," I'd told him glibly.

"I know you saw *something* one night," he put his cold hand on my shoulder, a cold I could feel through my shirt and sweater. He continued quietly. "Right now you are fighting every instinct you have just to stand here and return my gaze. I've seen that before. In many ways, you are not a *stranger* to me." He stepped back and put his shades on, smiled and walk over to his car.

"We'll talk later," he said and pulled away.

At the time, I had the cop's business card in my desk. I thought briefly about Jeffrey Dahmer, a serial killer I had seen on a documentary one night. After they caught on to this guy, the police found body parts in his locker at a candy factory where he had worked. I spend hours thinking about using my passkey to check out Strobos's locker but I didn't. He had been right, I was curious. I had already embarked on a strange trip and would make the night keep its wild promise no matter where it lead. He didn't have to take me in to his confidence, In some way, I was already in.

I was apprehensive an hour or so later because the police were back. I was worried Strobos would return and think that I'd finked. I was relieved for a fleeting moment when the detectives told me they came about Ronny Kolodny. Then they hit me with the news. He had been found dead in his apartment, hanging upside down in his closet with his throat slit. They showed me the photo and I reached for my cigarettes.

This time they were serious, they wanted something. In their thinking, they were at the garage once on a tip from Kolodny, and now Kolodny was dead. I gave them the owner's number. I showed them the locker with the news clippings taped to it and told them I wouldn't sleep right until they came back with a search warrant to tear the place apart in the morning.

I promised the complete cooperation of my guys on nights and gave the police my home number should anything come up. I followed them as they had a look around and when the opportunity arose, zealously tossed aside anything that got in their way. Another hour like that and we all would have gone out for drinks together.

Finally, I was relieved when they were gone and was totally unprepared for the rest of the night's pace.

Santos and his brother, Santos, were back. They were a bit short of their quotas but I didn't care. They parked and sat at the break table with fried eggs, white rice, pink beans and some creamy goat milk to pour over it all.

Strobos came back and passed me his little manilla envelope with the night's cash. I pulled it out and divided it out of habit. I took out his share which he and quite a few others liked at the end of their shifts. That's how I did it for illegal aliens and the like.

The rest of the income would be reported as mine even though I haven't driven in years. "Can you take a break, go out and get coffee or something?" he asked, quite innocently. I left the older Santos on the phones and got into D. Strobos's car around 3:30 AM. We drove to the Neptune, an all night diner near the Triborough Bridge.

"The police were in tonight. They were asking about Ronnie Kolodny. He's been murdered," I'd said.

"Is that what you're interested in, you care so much about Ronnie Kolodny?"

"No... But the police do. They're certain they're on to something. They're going to tear the garage apart," I told him. The waiter came by to take our order as Strobos pulled his pocket watch out. He considered the dial then snapped it shut and ordered.

"I'd like four eggs raw. And tabasco sauce." I asked for an Irish Coffee.

"Do you think it's wise to go flashing that around?"

"My watch?"

"The braid: Souvenirs are a bad risk, don't you think?" He laughed at me.

"You are a vile sort of man aren't you, Grislundt?"

"You think I'm vile? You? I saw you the other night, the girl in the trunk. You're the serial killer the police are looking for, and if you're picking them from the personals or chat rooms they will catch up with you real soon...Or if you have a weird thing about tattoos..."

He laughed some more. The waiter came back with our order.

"I'm no serial killer," he said.

"Oh, OK I'm sorry. Spree killer," I corrected.

"I'm no criminal. When a lion takes down a doe is that a crime? I'm disappointed. I really thought you were more observant."

"What did I miss? That you wear the same clothes everyday or that you sleep in the old heap in the garage?" I asked boldly.

"You really are a vile man, wretched to some extent."

"I'm vile and wretched?"

"A vile man cares not for his life or anyone else's. That's why you haven't told the authorities about me," he explained.

"So, in your opinion, apathy is more evil than murder."

"I told you, I do not murder anymore than the lion that takes down the doe, or the bear on its haunches devouring the fatty skin of live salmon," he doused the raw eggs with tabasco, stirred them and slurped half the viscous mixture down.

"So you view these girls as prey?" I asked. On his belt was a metal loop that held his slim stainless steel thermos. He detached it and put it down in front of me.

"Tomato soup?" I questioned.

"Go ahead," he nodded at the thermos. I took it, opened it and poured the rich red fluid into the little cup that fit on top. It wasn't tomato soup. I reached for my cigarettes with shaky hands and Strobos smiled. The bastard actually had one of his victim's blood with him. I wanted to step out and smoke, calm down and regain my usual perspective but there wasn't much time left before we needed to be back at the garage. I peered out at the comforting minutiae of the night, briefly then stepped back in and took my seat.

"I see the scars on your face Mr. Grislundt. I know where scars like that come from, I know how they are made," he'd said indicating the markings on my temple and over my eye made by my ex-wife years ago.

"I extend to you some measure of understanding. Everyone has a problem with women but you don't go around killing them and drinking their blood in a little fucking cup like some kind of.  vampire,"  At this he smiled even wider, bearing his astonishing canines.

"You don't expect me to believe you're some kind of inhuman creature that feeds on blood, some kind of Dracula thing, just because you found a sick dentist. I've read about freaks like you on the internet. You've got a major problem and I don't need to hear anything else. Let's get back to the garage. If the police get you, I don't want to know a fucking thing. It's none of my business." I got up went outside and lit my cigarette finally.

Through the glass, I could see him pay the check. I really began thinking I was in trouble, that I might end up prison with the sick freak because I had known something and said nothing, withheld information. A girl was possibly dead and I had kept the telltale shoe heel I'd found in his trunk. If he killed again, I was certainly morally if not criminally responsible.

Bad people had passed through the garage before, graceful as swans in a safe haven. I'd usually tip them off if I saw trouble brewing. They'd just move along, disappear. I didn't need their complications.

The elevated train nearby pulled noisily into the station above as Strobos came out of the diner.

"I need you to believe me, to believe *in* me. And you, you need to believe because your life may depend on it," he'd said and stepped past me into the black car.

Paralyzed and fearful, I sat there as he drove back through Astoria and told me his story. He told me he had been exposed to the blood of an immortal almost a thousand years ago.

Strobos used the word exposed because he regarded vampirism to be a disease like cancer. Once a human's cells are completely replaced by vampiric cells, the host can only continue by ingesting human blood or marrow cells. Contrary to folklore, he explained that only certain people would become vampires upon drinking the blood of another vampire. If he had more access to scientific research, he could probably link it to blood type or a genetic trait.

He told me the legends of a vampire's strength were related to the blood he or she consumed. The blood of the living was the most preferred for providing a vampire with superhuman strength and what he called the rare abilities. These included hypnotic powers, the ability to blend into one's surroundings, passing through walls and limb regeneration. Strobos didn't have any of those, very few vampires did. The blood from a fresh kill was OK for sustenance and nothing more. The blood of the cold dead wasn't deadly to a vampire as the lore went, just of no use.

Women's monthly secretions were good, ripe with potentiality, but had hallucinogenic side effects. In Ancient times, well meaning vampires would form many relationships with women in order to maintain a steady supply of this crazy blood. Unfortunately, the resulting flamboyant and often psychotic behavior would give them away as the beasts they were. Most of these relatively harmless types, known as the *Temenos Philia*, were massacred by the superstitious, if not jealous masses of the day.

The blonde watch fob was a souvenir but not the kind I'd thought. He told me that it was the hair of the woman he was to marry. In the sixteenth century, he was in love with a beauty named Demetra Tollis, whom he had exposed to his own blood in order to have her as a mate for all eternity. He'd taken one of her braids after she had been beheaded right in front of him by her older brother and uncle. He had escaped.

When it was convenient, Strobos had been searching for another woman to take her place ever since.

In the periods of subsequent loneliness and despair, he'd spent the better part of the past five hundred years in the dark safety of French and other European dungeons in the dank solitary pits for the murderously insane. There, grizzly killings were commonplace and often overlooked so he could feed when necessary and never see the light of day. If his age ever came into question it was thought to have been the result of the previous staff's poor penmanship. For hundreds of years, he had been taunted by Demetra's image in his dreams. She'd appear at a distance, make him chase her into a volcano of molten sunlight that would destroy everything it touched.

It all seemed like the obvious fantasy of a psychopath, but I had listened. Reverberating in my head at the time was the only thing he spoke which I felt was an absolute certainty; a vile man cares not for his life nor anyone else's. It was true. As I sat there with this maniac at the wheel, I realized I no longer cared for my life. Death was the wild potential I sought of the night, my own death.

I had tried to kill my wife after suspecting her of cheating, I had no tangible proof, just a feeling. She never forgave me, divorced me, took everything she could get and in my guilt I had willfully let it all go. Our friends had all taken her side and disowned me. Her brother had beaten me in the street and I had lain there in anticipation of the merciful killing blow that never came.

If D. Strobos was a vampire and was killing just to live and to love, I was more vile than this inhuman beast. It was hard to swallow, but there was a sense to it.

I hadn't noticed when the car stopped. We were in the queue of black and yellow medallion cars that were picking up passengers outside a club called BLIS near Queensboro Plaza.

"Crouch down low," he said, "I know you need this." He threw his dark pinstripe blazer over my head and I ducked out of sight below dash level as a young club patron hopped into the car. She didn't notice me, not because I wasn't noticeable but because she wasn't looking for me to be there. She had come from Forest Hills earlier in the evening and was heading back home alone for the night. Strobos checked his watch then adjusted his rearview mirror to get a look at his fare. She was about twenty three or so, clad in tight black leathers and a short green faux fur, black hair and gray eyes. She didn't have ideally attractive features but had been stunning overall in her evening makeup and tipsy grin.

Stopped at a light, Strobos spoke to her in Russian. Surprised, she laughed at whatever he'd said and spoke to him. She also spoke Croatian and some German. Strobos proved to be equally witty in both. In English, he told her his shift was almost over and wondered if she would mind if he stopped quickly at an all night drive through carwash before getting on the expressway. Just down the street, he pointed to it and promised to give her a break on the fare.

Strobos made a derogatory remark about what a Nazi his dispatcher was and they laughed some more.

We pulled into the all night automated car wash on Northern Boulevard that usually does our cars. When the first blast of sudsy water blurred the world away, he turned up the radio playing throbbing techno club music.

"Enjoy the show," he'd said in English which I realized was directed at me. Almost frenetically, rollers and brushes assaulted the car. In a streak of darkness, Strobos leapt over the front bench at the passenger, landed between her legs, tore open her jacket and blouse in one motion as she screamed. More horrible fuzzy rollers and jets of water impacted loudly.

The struggle was brief, he had taken both wrists and held them pinned away at arms length, his jaw clamped down relentlessly upon her pale throat with alien savagery as wild patterns of foam and water washed over them both.

When the hot air dryers came on, he was back in the driver's seat. His animal-like tongue licked blood from his face and chin before he pulled out of the car wash and paid the attendant.

We had sped away then entered a parking lot outside a dark and shuttered strip of shops.

Strobos tossed the body out on the ground, pale breast and shoulders splotched with blood, steaming in the cold. He wiped most of the blood off the car seats with her faux fur then tossed that aside as well.

I watched the sparse traffic flash pass us, wondering if the police would show.

Strobos pulled me over near the corpse and made me watch him take the head off as easily as one might tear a hunk of bread off a French loaf. He lobbed it on top of the nearest shop's roof and we sped off again.

I told him that murder and decapitation didn't prove anything supernatural and at that instant the car swerved and skidded out in front of an oncoming vehicle which stopped abruptly in order to avoid collision.

D. Strobos opened his door, streaked skyward to disappear from sight for a moment and then landed cat-like on the big SUV in front of us. He kicked the windshield in. Two passengers climbed out, one brandishing the long bar of an old steering wheel lock. Strobos jumped down on the opposite side of the truck and flipped it over on the two men with considerable ease.

Having witnessed the impossible and the insane made me feel like I was living inside a dream. I kept looking for clues in the dark sky and little details, the telltale signs of the unreal, but there were none but Strobos himself.

Cautiously, he drove us back to the garage. His eyes were a terrible bloodshot red after feeding. I guess it explained the dark glasses he often wore.

When we got out, he looked at his watch and the purple gray of twilight and then to me as if to ask if the last fifteen minutes had dispelled my disbelief. I had slowly nodded in affirmation then called out to him as he was about to walk away.

"What about those eggs? Vampires eat eggs?"

"They're good for the hair, nails and skin. If you ever see another of us and they really look like shit, they're not eating their eggs," he explained as a tiny muted chime in his watch alerted him to the impending sunrise. Inside the garage, he walked over to the old Lincoln and climbed into the trunk to lie on his precious native soil.

I looked for a bottle of Armor-All and a roll of brown paper towels and clean the car's vinyl upholstery, thinking about daylight.

Apparently it was one part of the vampire folklore which held true.

I tried to approach it from a scientific standpoint. Lots of creatures on this planet are affected by sunlight. Some people even got skin cancer and died.

When finally home in broad daylight, I realized I still had blood on my hands, under my nails, in the creases of my fingers. I washed them, trembling my cigarette ashes onto the suds. I drew the shades and put on the TV. I poured myself a double cognac in a coffee mug, plopped some honey in, put it in the microwave and waited for the ready beeps.

As I settled under the blanket and slurped hot booze, I thought about what else Strobos had said earlier. Something about my life depending on what I witnessed. I searched the blood, the fangs, the scream and dead empty eyes in my memory. Did a buck just watch as a lion tore a doe apart? Strobos was a vampire and I was a vile and horrible human being. I shook with awful laughter as the alcohol cradled my brain in its grave mirth.

*"Doe a deer a female deer, ray a drop of golden sun..."* I sang and drifted off as the news related the story of the latest headless victim.

About three hours later, there was a knock at my door. I usually ignore these and they go away. The knocker kept getting louder, practically banging. I dragged myself over to the door and it swung open as soon as I unlocked it. Two men in crappy suits and overcoats barged in past me. The bigger of the two was Detective Emmet Long, the cop I spoke to a couple of nights ago. He was stocky and tall, vaguely fifty and vaguely non-Caucasian. His close cropped salt and pepper hair sparkled in the sunlight that stabbed my little studio from the spaces around my window shades. The other was a shorter Asian man who looked around the room silently.

"Grislundt, Trevor, M. What were you doing last night?" Long asked.

"Work. You know the place. Dos Primos Car Service on 55th."

"Did you leave your post after 4AM for any reason."

"I took a break and had an Irish Coffee at the Neptune Diner."

His partner sniffed the coffee cup that I dropped near the sofa this morning. He frowned and shook his head.

"Anyone see you there or on the way?"

"I went with a co-worker, Dion Strobos. We left and returned sometime before dawn," I told them.

"Where is he now?"

"I can't say what any man does after his shift, but I'll bet he's asleep like I was." And then I realized that the red shoe heel was still on the table in my ash tray.

"Now that I'm up, do you gentlemen mind if I smoke?" I said, slightly mimicking Humphrey Bogart.

"Go ahead," Long said. I stood between them and the table. Discreetly, I stuffed the red spike in my cigarette pack then took one out and lit it. Luckily, there were only four or five left in the box.

"I don't know if you've seen the news yet. There's been another killing, the same M.O. It happened on your shift not too far from Dos Primos," he said indicating my TV which then featured some reality show teen crap.

"I must have missed it."

"I hope so. We're going to check out your coffee story and that Strobe...Strobo guy's as well.

Young women travel by taxi at night. In the next couple of days, we are going to tear the garage apart. We have to wait for the official post mortem from the coroner and check another few items out, but we'll be there," Long said.

"You know where to find me."

"I'd better," Long finished. His quiet sidekick considered me skeptically for a moment then filed out behind him.

There had been a subdued tension in the air later that night. Jackie French saw me come in. He hung up on his old lady without all the sappy terms of affection and left almost immediately. Three driver's hadn't shown up so we were short staffed and I had to keep the lines on hold until someone was free. Strobos had said nothing unusual to me at all until 2AM or so when he reported dropping a fare in Manhattan and was bound for the 59th Street Bridge. He also described a dream he'd had, a nightmare by my standards. In it, he was falling through the sky over field of jagged wooden spikes.

When I asked why the wooden spikes he explained, "A wooden spike to the heart would kill anyone, the blunter the better, the more damaging. Sharp metal would make wounds which would heal and seal up neatly in a vampire strong with fresh blood."

It still seemed so unreal. Like many forays into the night, certainty and tangibility seemed to dissipate in daylight. Phantoms grew pale, lost in the sky blue wash of mornings, grind of weekday traffic, the clean hair and caffeine jitters of commuters, the welcoming cocoon of commerce, the attractive strut of the hopeful.

A witness to murder and mayhem, and I had really felt no different. Sure, I had been concerned about the police, but overall, it was exciting. I was in touch with something beyond humanity. In my late twenties, I had been a member of SETI; the Search for Extra Terrestrial Intelligence. I had always hoped to find something else in the universe which would put an end to all the wondering and conjecture. This wasn't what I had in mind, but oh yes, there was a rush.

I went in early, just before sunset and sat on the trunk of the old Lincoln and waited. I hoped down at the first sign of movement. Strobos got out of the trunk quite unceremoniously and brushed soil off his suit. I asked him about the dirt. He said it was a tradition or something more akin to superstition. No vampire needed special Transylvanian dirt but it seemed everyone needed something that said home in some way.

I was familiar with the term *familiar* from the vampire genre movies I'd seen as a child. A vampire's familiar always seemed to live in the vampire's lair to watch over the coffin during the day. I wondered why Strobos didn't have a hip pad in Manhattan or Brooklyn even. I had begun to fantasize about planning incredible robberies he could commit in order for us to finance a great condo or loft. He could use money to attract women instead of searching in the classified ads and on Craigslist. I could organize orgies with the rejects. I was envisioning dark stonework, a six foot tall roaring fireplace, lots of cushions strewn about. I considered dressing in black and dyeing my hair.

In the hour before dawn, Strobos had burst my bubble. He had come rolling in after my break. When he told me about having only one more date from the personals, I thought he was ending the spree of killings to lay low and start playing it smart. Strobos meant something entirely different.

He was giving up. Strobos had been trying to replace a woman he hadn't seen in hundreds of years. Finding attractive women he liked or reminded him of Demetra then having to destroy them if things didn't work out, was far too depressing to continue. He was tired of the dreams and the running.

This sullen creature told me of desperate strands of eternity wherein he had simply stood still for years at a time in dusty, forgotten mid western bomb shelters, European catacombs and subterranean arctic caverns.

A vampire's familiar is always a wretched individual. That is apparently the basis of selection but like everything else in nature it constituted an efficient program of divine equilibrium.

Whenever I think back to that windy Westchester evening, attempted murder, my short term in a state institution, I have cause to wonder. Had I stopped short of killing my wife because of morals or love, or was it that I had been afraid of fucking it up somehow and not getting away with it? I choose to believe the latter. I couldn't carry out the attempted murder without ruining my life, so I'm sure I would have botched an actual murder, which is why I didn't know if I could help Strobos when he told me what he had wanted.

If this last young woman didn't work out, he'd planned to fast for three days and have me destroy him.

Now, I sit on the roof of the garage before sunrise. It didn't matter much. We were closed. Under the stress of the investigation, my illegals, bail jumpers and deadbeat dads all took a powder. Several of our cars have been impounded for all sorts of reasons because the police had found traces of a victim's blood in one of them.

The last woman Strobos called had made a date with him to pick her up at a club called Downtime. Downtime had a small stage and on certain nights crowds of gothic music fans congregated in black, leather and shiny vinyl. She was one of these, a bright college girl named Lauren. They watched a band called Unto Ashes for thirty minutes or so.

She had black hair that was golden at the roots, black lipstick, green eyes and leather. After three encounters, he sprung it on her. At first, he'd said she didn't believe him but thought it was fun and sexy. He convinced her to take some X scored at the club. She allowed him to drink some of her blood from a tiny bite on her shoulder and she then drank his blood from a similar bite. When the drug wore off,

Strobos jumped out of the window from her twelfth floor apartment then calmly knocked on the door, unharmed less than 5 minutes later.

He'd said she was excited, so many of the gothic music fans were fascinated or even obsessed with the idea of vampirism. She resumed writing the poetry she had started to write in high school - Then, the young woman started to pierce every possible appendage of her body, letting him drink the drops of blood she'd shed. When the transformation was complete her personality changed drastically. She had killed her roommate then tore her apart. Strobos knew she would be one of the insane prowling horrors, an entity on a rampage ripping through the night with an insatiable blood lust. He'd seen it before and didn't want to be responsible for one of those. With a long blade from her kitchen, he had beheaded her. Instead of drinking her blood, he had staked her with a broken broom handle then kissed her lips one more time before lobbing her head out of the window in a violent twist of rage and despair.

We the wretched are selected, either to be made more wretched by hosting and aiding a bloodthirsty beast or we could be redeemed to some extent by being given the chance to destroy one, potentially saving the thousands who'd fall prey over the course of a several human lifetimes. Would my life turn around after knowing I had done some good in the world? Would I forgive myself and leave my guilt and my murky private limbo behind?

We angled our beach chairs to the brighter horizon. Strobos gave me his pocket watch and I opened it and stooped to stand it between us on the pebble flecked tar of the roof. I had tied several cinderblocks to his arms and legs. We were waiting patiently.

I looked at the watch. It was almost seven. I could see the first golden curls of sun in the tiny window of the watch's sky dial as the first fine halo of red swelled from the horizon. I saw something in his bloodless eyes akin to panic. I gently put his sunglasses on which calmed him a bit, reminded him of the enterprise at hand.

He told me his latest dream. It had been Demetra as usual, they were falling into a fiery brilliance, tumbling over and over. Perhaps they were falling into the sun, perhaps they were falling into hell. No one's dreams really made complete sense.

"Maybe you will spend eternity with her after all," I'd said, "You made her a vampire. She fed on innocent life. If there is a god, maybe you'll see her in hell," I added in an awkward attempt to be comforting.

"Yes. Maybe I'll see her in Hell," he said, making me hear the capital H.

# 2

# DRIFTER

## 2006

Snow had fallen sometime in the night and the cold wind blew tiny crystals through the air stinging my face as I pedaled in the predawn darkness. It was a cool bleak April, the world seemed alien and empty to me.

Odd things were going on at work and the feeling that something was wrong seemed to permeate my life.

I live in a town without a name, not even a town really, a few strips of prefab buildings that sprung up around the new KwikiTrak service station near the highway between Harrisburg and Leola. The Post Office gave us our own zip code for the narrow wedge of forest, road and new concrete to be addressed simply as KwikiTrak, Pennsylvania.

A hydraulic brake screamed in the distance from somewhere off the shoulder beyond the wooded glade as it did almost every morning without fail. Trucks meant work. I used to thank god every time I heard a rig take our exit but in the last three years or so I started to hate them. I knew they'd all come in eventually and I'd have to cook up their griddle cakes and sausages, their four egg omelets, greasy mounds of bacon and home-fries.

I didn't hate my old man although everyone says I should have. I was living this nightmare almost as a direct result of his foolishness. While I was finishing high school, he started to drink because my mother was a cheat.

We lived by the railroad outside of Scranton and she had started to screw around with one of the O'Neill twins whose family practically ran the town back then. My dad had come back from a three day stint out east and found out where Todd O'Neill liked to flop.

Intoxicated and mad as hell, he leveled the little cottage with his semi. Unfortunately, he found Terry O'Neill, the other brother. He was wasting away in prison for killing the wrong man. I felt real bad for him, not being able to do his time with the satisfaction of knowing he was there paying for something he had meant to do. He and Terry had actually been friends briefly in childhood. Every month, when I bring his cartons of Pall Malls, he would just sit there shaking his head, trying not to weep.

My mother had stayed around long enough to dump me on my granddad who died four months later while I was making him dinner. He was tuned into his favorite program, *Bay Watch*. I had just fried up some bologna, onions and cheese for him when I heard his rocker slowly cease its squeak. I ate the greasy lunch meat on toast with a dead man I hardly knew, watched big boobed blondes bounce on the beach then packed my shit and took off.

It's been eight years of washing cars, chopping firewood and flipping burgers. When I interviewed for the short order cook spot here at the KwikiTrak, the frog faced old prick who hired me had slapped my back hard and commented that he could practically smell the cooking fat on me when I walked in the door. Of course, I wanted the position but that didn't stop me from wanting to throttle this jerk because he thought I belonged here.

If the job hadn't come with a small studio apt in the modern prefab units at the end of the strip, I probably would have told him to fuck himself then moved on.

I slowed down a bit. Up ahead was the spot where I'd ran into some raccoon carcasses just yesterday. I actually rolled into the mess and slid in a pile of entrails, nearly fell off my bicycle in it. This morning they were gone, probably dragged into the woods by other less dangerous critters than the one that killed them. It was weird, made unforgettable because of the way they had been ripped open and left side by side.

I was coming up on the pumping station where Tong worked. He's a young Korean who lives in the apartment above me, a hard working guy, always pulling doubles. He was saving money to bring his family to Jersey next year. He waved to me, I nodded and pedaled on.

I could see my least favorite rig in the lot already. It was Burke, a guy from Dallas who I secretly refer to as Burke the Jerk. He liked his scrambled eggs loose but not runny. It was a fine line located no where in reality. I cooked them the same every time but he'd send them back intermittently, especially on the days when I really looked tired.

In the shadow dropping from the KwikiTrak Grill's awning was the real wild card. In a dark hooded sweatshirt and pinstripe slacks, starring blankly up at the evergreens swaying in the early darkness, was the Drifter.

I'd seen his type come and go. Long haired city boys in thrift shop clothing and surplus military boots. They come out 'round our way trying to get some of real America to rub off on 'em. They seemed to think being a little dirty around the edges and hanging out amongst the desolate could somehow bring greater depth to their lives. They were always would be poets, actors or musicians. Nowadays, some of them think they could be Andy Warhols just because they have a laptop computer. As far as I could tell, they were just a bunch of pussies who never amounted to anything. Easily bored and unable to be away from the cold massive teats of their metropolitan hubs, they never stayed, only passed through looking down on us while trying to be chummy. You know the type. They always felt obliged to use the names stitched on our uniforms or embossed on our plastic name tags. They loved older motorcycles, strange radios or anything that was deemed *vintage*.

This guy was a bit different. He was definitely city, but made no efforts at being particularly friendly or interested in the details of our nitty gritty shitty lives when he first dragged himself in here a few mornings ago. I'll have to admit, I didn't mind him for a customer, he only ordered raw eggs with tabasco sauce then sat silently reading the local papers. Just before the sun was in the sky, he'd crawl back to whatever rock he hid under.

His face didn't look old, but there was the sense of very long unpleasant years in his eyes. He seemed beaten down, broken or injured internally. He moved slowly and cautiously.

Peggy, one of the wait staff, had decided he was a drug addict because he had shown up yesterday in shades and had a little more pep in his step.

Peggy Weiszinski is a big Polish woman originally from the Bronx, whose husband and daughter had been killed on September 11, 2001. They were shopping in the World Trade Center Mall not too far from where Mr. Weiszinski had worked. They were crushed by hot falling debris while trying to get back to the subway with Peggy's birthday gifts. In her early fifties, she's bitter, sarcastic on a good day and just very negative overall. I didn't blame her. I understood that there were things in life you just didn't get over. The woman was just a few Smirnoff's from being a complete alcoholic but never missed a shift, goofed an order or dropped a dish.

When hungover her pale skin was pink and we all knew better to approach her at least until sun up. She had offered the Drifter a free coffee in sympathy for whatever his sickly condition was the first time he came in and he turned it down, making her shit list immediately.

So far, the only one he talked to was Didi, a young black chick from Philly who worked the counter. I had mistaken her for a foreigner at first, her skin was much darker than most African Americans and her face was sharp and jewel like. She had the kind of figure I've mostly seen on young black women; voluptuous and athletic at the same time. Didi had just turned twenty two in February and was on probation for fraud and identity theft. She had worked at a restaurant further east and borrowed the occasional customer's credit card digits. Everyone paid in cash at this shit hole so there was no worry about a repeat performance.

In the plate glass, I could see Burke the Jerk slurping coffee, teetering back and forth on his boot heels, waiting for me. The idea that a greedy, obnoxious, fat prick like this might salivate when he saw me, made me sick. I flipped him the bird as usual and he just jiggled and giggled. He knew I couldn't do a damn thing about having to slave over the grill for him at five AM.

Peggy was setting places at the counter when I walked in. Doug, the night cook was lacing up his leathers when I walked into the locker room.

"Jimmy B! How's it hanging?" he lisped at me, missing front teeth.

"Same old, same old," I mumbled and leaned my bike against the lockers.

"Your freak show is still going on. Peggy says she spotted that city guy jonesing in the woods when she had her first smoke."

"Like either of you should talk, Reefer- man," I kidded him.

"Nothing wrong with a little smoke. I ain't a zombie like that dude." He got up and grabbed his helmet.

"Take it easy," I said.

"You know it, Bro'. I'm going home, banging my old lady. I'm gonna smoke up and watch the cartoon channel 'til I pass out."

I heard his cycle Doppler off into the distance. A few moments later, I tied on my apron and went out front to the kitchen to deal with Burke's breakfast.

A good buddy of Burke's came in and sat at his table. Between the two, they ordered enough food for a family of six to eat buffet style. While Peggy carried out their eggs and bacon, the Drifter quietly entered.

I noticed he never wanted to be the only customer in the joint. He sat at his usual table, closest to the door. Through the wavy heat coming up off the grill, I could see Burke and his buddy commenting to each other and smirking.

The moment I knew would come materialized before my eyes. Someone decided to fuck with him.

Burke's good buddy threw a tiny foil pack of jam at the lone stranger. It hit him on the head and landed in front of him on his newspaper. He picked it up and examined it for a moment. He got up, silencing the laughter at the other table. Peggy, hands on hips, watched disapprovingly as he approached the truckers. Didi came in from the back with a tray of freshly filled ketchup squeeze bottles.

"Hey Dion. The usual, bloody eggs?" she asked brightly, referring to his tabasco spiced raw eggs which she imagined as a type of hangover helper like a Bloody Mary. He nodded then stood over the truckers and held out the little packet of jam.

"It seems you gents dropped this," he said quietly. Burke stuffed food in his face and chewed blankly with his mouth open. "Uh...thanks," The other trucker said becoming shy all of a sudden.

It was a situation I haven't seen since grade school. The cutest girl in the room addressed the stranger by his first name and the pecking order was changed. Her small approbation was enough to diffuse the situation. Burke and his buddy have stolen glances at Didi, even leered if they were lucky enough to catch her bending over, but never really socialized with anyone but Peggy who was closer to their age and a charming eyesore even on her best days.

The Drifter dropped the packet on the table.

"I wouldn't want you to miss your fruity spread," he said then walked up to the counter and looked over the grill at me for a moment. I had been chewing a wad of overcooked bacon. I smirked and shook my head.

"You oughta try soft boiled with a little bacon and toast. It's good and you could still spice it up," I suggested.

Two more customers came in. He went back to his table near the door. I cooked and cooked. From time to time, I noticed Didi hanging out with him, making quiet small talk. It got busier and before I knew it, the sun was up and Dion the Drifter was gone.

I fried my way through the eight o'clock rush then took my break. I had put orange juice, apple juice, ice, a banana and a raw egg in the blender then stood outside sipping. After serving raw eggs these days, I decided to throw a few into my own diet. It seemed healthy.

I looked into the restaurant at the broad backs of the two remaining customers hunched over their dishes at the counter. One displayed a few more inches of ass crack than the law should allow and I wished Peggy would say something to the pig.

In the last year or so, I really started to hate the people I cooked for. I still did a good job. I that did for myself.

Before returning to the grill, I found Didi sitting at what we all started to think of as the Drifter's table. Her head was bopping softly. There were tiny white plugs in her ears.

"Hey Didi, what you got there?" I asked.

"A group called *Massive Attack*," she said, a bit too loudly.

"I mean, where did you get that audio player?" I said referring to the small white cube with a bright LED readout on the side.

"Dion gave it to me. Isn't he something!" she said becoming childishly shrill with excitement.

"I wouldn't get hooked to people just passing through," I suggested, hoping not to sound jealous. Then over my shoulder came the blast of an outraged "*What!*" from Peggy, who apparently caught the last segment of our little talk.

"You stay the hell away from that sick drug freak, young lady! And don't you dare start taking his gifts and money. You shouldn't even go near him. You keep to the counter customers and leave the floor to me. Men like that can only drag you down," Peggy warned, her face beet red.

"How much lower can I sink than this place? And how 'bout when you got those free sneakers to send to your nephew? What do say now?" Didi countered.

"That was different. This is not a dance hall and you are not a dance hall girl!"

"What? What the hell does that mean? Why don't you say what you really mean? Why don't you say what you really mean? You're not my mother, just an old drunk!"

I knew what to do from experience. They went on like that for awhile entertaining the two wretches at the counter while I went downstairs to drag up another sack of potatoes, another sack of big Spanish onions.

Everything blew over by ten. Customers came and went, I cleaned up and waited on the occasional trooper who stopped in for fritters and coffee. I heard the second shift cook at the kitchen door behind me. Finally, I could go back home.

Although the apartment was new, the way it was furnished made it look dingy. It seemed the management stretched every dime 'til Roosevelt screamed murder. The whole building was filled with miss matched smelly shit culled from thrift shops, garage sales and what I believe to have been shameless dumpster diving.

I hung a poster and got a small TV but the reception was terrible without cable.

At some point in the marvelous afternoon, Tong Muhn dropped off a little package for me. He was always bringing me his leftovers, but I could hardly ever eat whatever it was supposed to be.

Apparently, he'd been to Harrisburg and found a Korean or a Korean Deli. He left me some kimchee and bibimbop or something like that. I tried some of the meat and eggs then flushed the rest because the last time it was in my trash can the smell gave me nightmares. I'm sure there is something I can eat from Korea but it definitely wasn't going to be spicy raw radishes. I understood much of so called peasant cuisine consisted of things poor people could afford but when it became possible to eat better elsewhere, why wouldn't they?

I showered and bicycled to Leola to visit their public library. I browsed the old CD collection hoping to find some *Velvet Underground* or *Nico*. Doug had played me an old song called *Venus in Furs* and I was hooked. They had some Lou Reed, but nothing I was interested in. There was a CD by *Massive Attack*. Curious, I borrowed it and a collection of instrumentals released by David Bowie called *All Saints*.

I listened to the *Massive Attack* on my headphones while pedaling back on lone side streets. It was atmospheric stuff from the late 90's often described by music magazines as trip hop. It could definitely be called drug music; produced for the listening pleasure of people who get stoned by people who get stoned. If that was the kind of thing the Drifter was passing to Didi, maybe Peg was right and the Drifter was into drugs after all but this was only music.

It was after dusk when I rolled into the KwikiTrak complex. There was an unusual amount of police cars in the lot at the restaurant. Getting closer, I recognized the deputy sheriff's cruiser. Deputy Barry Tiltson had a miniature black and gold Steelers helmet lodged into his dash. He wasn't a bad guy as far as lawmen went. On the job for more than twenty years, Tiltson seemed only to be interested in football and retirement. The other cars were State Troopers.

Tempted as I was to stop in and see what was going on, I hated to going near the place before my shift started. I passed close enough to see inside but only learned they weren't sitting at a table chewing the fat.

Something must have happened on the highway or maybe they sought leads on a fugitive. It wouldn't be the first time. The Drifter came to mind immediately.

I wondered if the third shift's crew would give him up then wondered how much they really knew about him. Doug, the cook, was an ex-con. He probably wouldn't say anything but I didn't really know about the others, they were new and I didn't know how much gossiping went on about things that happened on the overnight.

I went back home. If they wanted to talk to me it could wait until I was on the payroll. I tossed and turned. I knew they would talk to me. I knew they wanted something and they were dragging old Barry Tiltson around to get in smooth with the locals. So long on the job, he knew us all.

Old Barry has been known to catch people in lies simply because he's lived and worked amongst them for so long.

I'd met him after the paper pushers at the KwikiTrak did my criminal history check through his office. When he saw my last name, Tiltson decided to look me up claiming to have known my grandparents but never said how.

Certain of not knowing anything about anything, I don't know why I was anxious. It was just a bad feeling I had been having and couldn't honestly say it had anything to do with Dion the Drifter, but he was the only new variable in our lonely dead end sagas.

A Spring storm woke me when I finally managed to fall asleep. Exhausted, I took a hot shower and dressed. According to the news, the temperature had dropped 15 degrees. I bundled up then topped it all off with a flimsy rain poncho from my high school years.

The rains had ended by the time I was pedaling. Fog hid everything but the lights and tall trees lining the road. The storm had passed save for an occasional distant flash and rumble.

Mind full of Barry Tiltson and the Drifter, I was distracted. The poor visibility and my poncho's hood were also to blame.

There was an access lane for people who got off on the wrong exit and wanted to get back on the highway. It was old and bumpy, improperly maintained. Weeds shot up belligerently in the cracked asphalt.

I thought I saw something out of the corner of my eye, an impossible floating orb. I turned and pedaled towards the spot I believed it to be but it was gone. I got off the bike and stepped into the woods. Everything was so damp, branches bent instead of snapping, making it difficult to find a fresh path if there really had been one left in the orb's wake. I was certain something was moving in the thick growth from the sound of wet rustling but I couldn't see anything.

Dumbfounded, I got back on my bike and went to work.

Before I could say anything about my UFO sighting, I saw Peggy standing outside the lady's restroom. I could hear someone vomiting violently inside. Didi came out drenched in perspiration, spent looking. "Rough night?" I offered, looking at her oddly bloodshot eyes. Peggy was so worried she was speechless for a change and I didn't blame her. Didi looked awful. She was pale or something. Her espresso bean smooth complexion was unusually dull, ashy and almost what I might call gray. Her body seemed weakened, her muscles and flesh seemed to hang uselessly or incorrectly from her bones.

She claimed to feel a little better and couldn't be convinced to go home. Peggy had her lie down in the back where Doug was getting ready to leave.

In the midst of all this, the most comforting thing for me to do was follow my routine. I changed, washed my hands and started the home-fries. Doug came out into the kitchen "She looks like baked shit in there, Man. I've seen it all, but I never seen anyone look so bad. He must have given her some new synthetic shit," Doug said, his shaggy hair flying as he nodded over and over.

"He who?" I asked.

"That sick freak who comes in here sucking raw eggs, that's who!" Peggy interjected, her huge angry red head jutting through the order window connecting the kitchen to the dinning area.

"You don't know the latest, Jimmy. The fucking cops were in here," Doug said, still shaking his head.

"They came in with Barry last night asking questions. When they come to us today, I'm giving them that little bastard," she said.

"What makes you think he had something to do with her?" I asked.

"She told me they met once before her shift. They took a walk. He gave her some magazines and music and god know what else. If it's drugs, the police should know. If he's contaminated the poor girl somehow, he should be quarantined," she ranted.

"What are the police looking for?" I asked her.

"There was a killing. One of the Amish. I'll bet he robbed and killed someone. I'm telling them everything I know!" She stomped off in the direction of a couple of customers who had just come in.

Peggy was fuming, but what did she know? After hearing Didi hung out with the drifter, her estimation of him made some sense but what did it have to do with dead Amish guys. Party drugs and young girls didn't seem to mix with murder or the Amish, as far as I knew. And what did golf too proud for buttons have to rob anyway?

Didi couldn't keep anything down but tea. She was able to work for a while but by sun up she had a headache and felt weak. Peggy sent her back to the old cot in the locker room.

When the Drifter hadn't shown, his absence only made his guilt seem all the more certain. As I cracked eggs and flipped flapjacks, I kept an eye on the plate glass. I wanted to see him, I wanted to see if there was even a trace of concern for Didi who seemed to be in peril.

Peggy worked twice as hard and twice as fast. She was unusually reticent. She was either saving it all for the police, or perhaps she wanted a confrontation with Didi's new friend to find out what he had done to her. We checked on Didi just after ten. She was sleeping. Peggy had thrown a blanket over her because she was ice cold. If she hadn't stirred a bit we probably would have called 911 because she looked dead.

Deputy Tiltson had shown up in the lot ten minutes later. He looked terrible, probably from working 'round the clock. When the troopers came in, they sat at a table and ordered coffee with egg sandwiches. The troopers bused their table and loitered within earshot, not to miss anything.

Peggy made old Barry a large sweet iced coffee and he took a swig or two before getting down to business.

"I guess you both know why we're here," Tiltson said and then looked around.

"Where's your help, Peg?" he asked.

"Didi's not doing too well," Peggy answered trying to remain calm to gather her thoughts.

"She's napping in the back. She was sick all morning," I told him.

"Peter Dobbs on days, says there's an out of towner whose been hanging around on your shift. A guy with no luggage or vehicle who isn't local. I don't want anyone to be alarmed if you see him again. I just want you to call me. I need to ask him some questions, get some background on him. We have a killing on our hands and no real leads. I'm still waiting on forensics from Philly, but we are stumped." Tiltson told them.

"He's usually here earlier, Barry. Sits over there eating raw eggs and reading the classifieds. He didn't come in today because he knows better than to show his face after what he's done to Didi," Peggy accused.

"What exactly do you mean by that?" Tiltson asked looking to us both for answers.

"He's some kind of drug addict or drug pusher, and they've been together," Peggy accused.

"Now those are serious allegations, Peg. Did you see anything or did Didi say anything about drugs?" Tiltson asked, his face looking sadder and older by the second.

"No one's ever seen or said anything about drugs," I said, "but Didi doesn't look too good."

"You say she spent some time with him, maybe she could give us some idea about who he is. She's in the back? Lets have a look at her," Tiltson said. "You do realize if Didi is under the influence of or in the possession of a controlled substance or associating with a known felon, she's in violation of her probation and I would be obligated to make a report to her probation officer."

I made Didi another cup of tea and we walked to the back room to see her. Tiltson dropped to one knee and studied the sleeping girl for a moment. He gently checked her arms. There were no needle marks. Peggy woke Didi.

"The deputy's here. He's got some questions you need to answer," Peggy told her as she yawned and stretched.

"Hi Barry. Questions about what? You know I'm on probation," she said and took the tea from me.

"I'm looking to question one of your customers in connection with a crime which occurred not too far from here. Peg says you know him best, and maybe you can help us find him," Tiltson explained in as charming a manner as he could muster. Didi looked at us and back to Tiltson.

"You mean Dion?" she asked, looking directly at Peg.

"Dion? Do you know his last name?" Tiltson asked, pulling out his book. "We just want to talk with him. He's in no trouble as far as I know," he added as Didi turned to Peg glaring suddenly then hopped up off the cot.

"You just can't stand seeing me get with a white boy. I see the way you look at us!"

"You little bitch! I'm just trying to look out for you! Look at yourself. You're in here looking like a goddamn zombie, puking your guts out. Something foul is going on and that junkie creep is surely the cause!" Peggy stomped away to see if there were any new customers out front.

"Listen Didi, nobody cares how you spend your time or who you spend it with but if a crime is involved…" Tiltson started.

"We don't do anything like that!" She broke the ceramic mug in her hand spilling the tea and shaking away the fragments surprising all of us. Frightened, she held her hand close to examine it, trembling. Barry and I looked at each other speechlessly for a moment. I knew the mugs were old and some had fine hairline fractures from years of use and dishwashing but to see it crushed into fragments in Didi's small hand was freaky as all hell. She flopped back down on the cot shivering.

"I still don't feel too good," she said.

"Hey, wash up. You should go home and get some rest. Peg and I can handle it. I'll punch you out regular time," I said and winked at Barry.

"That sounds about right. You don't live here on the complex, do you?" Tiltson asked.

"She's over in Leola, right off the main drag," I said.

"I'm gonna give you a lift home young lady. Seems like you've had quite a day already," he said giving her shoulder a little rub. "I'm gonna have a word or two with Jimmy, just make yourself comfortable in my cruiser when you're ready. Sit in the front," Tiltson said to assure her it was just a friendly lift. Didi stepped into the bathroom and closed the door behind her. Tiltson dropped to the cot himself and exhaled a gust reeking of cigarettes, coffee and exhaustion.

"Something sure ain't right with that one," Tiltson said, "What's your take on it, Jimmy?"

"Hard to say. This guy, she calls Dion showed up four or five days ago, dragged himself in here, the walking dead. He's come in everyday since, except for today.

Comes in after 4:30AM or so when it's still dark. We didn't know what his story was and he isn't really much of a talker. He wears sunglasses at night. I know it isn't a crime but he's no pop star. Looks like he's from somewhere east. You know the type, funky vintage clothes and surplus military boots.

He's got balls though. Once, a couple of the yokels came in here and threw something at him and he got up, crossed the room and politely returned it to them. I'd thought I have to call you then but it blew over." "He's some kind of show off? A macho power trip chip on his shoulder?" Tiltson suggested.

"No. I don't think so. That's what made it odd enough to bring up. He practically staggers in like a frail broken thing but looked like he was ready to go at it with a couple of stupid truckers over a pack of jam."

"Showing off for the ladies?" Barry asked.

"It didn't seem so but he evidently had an effect on Didi," I answered recalling the scene. Tiltson blew his sorry breath at me again.

"What exactly happened out there, Barry?" I asked confidentially. He got up and looked down the corridor that led to the kitchen before he spoke.

"Two Amish brothers were over at that carton factory over on Hewlett. They had stocked their wagon and were returning to their farm."

"They're quite a ways from Amish country."

"Well, they have an account there. They normally have cartons shipped but it seems there was a bumper crop. Anyway, one brother got off the wagon to relieve himself au natural. When he returned minutes later, the other is sitting in the wagon dead with what looks like a bullet hole in his chest. Like I said before, I'm still waiting on forensics.

"Aint that some shit,"

"I'll say. And because it happened on the stretch of Hewlett that's really highway over there, I have these state dildos up my ass on it."

"I don't know what you'll hear from the others about this Dion guy but no one has seen or said anything about a gun," I told him.

"Yet you say he was willing to square off with a couple of fellows even as he appeared to be ill or injured or something?" Tiltson verified, eyebrows arched in interest. "That's right."

"You know I spoke with Douglas Tibits? He had nothing to say. I think he's holding a grudge." Tiltson said with a bit of a smirk. "He always wears his helmet now. I even think he likes it but won't admit it," I told him.

"I'm going out front to talk to the state boys for a bit," he said, gave me an avuncular slap on the shoulder, went out to the dining area to bring the troopers up to speed and save them from Peggy. I could hear her out there giving them quite an earful.

Didi came from the restroom and went to her locker. She sat down and changed into her street shoes which were a cleaner pair of glorified sneakers, their thick soles adorned with red and amber reflectors.

"Tiltson's out front," I told her.

"It's OK to ride with him, Jimmy?"

"It's fine. You know old Barry. He's a real straight arrow but doesn't want any complications. Never wants the job get too interesting, you know."

"OK."

"Are you planning to see...uh Dion? You know I won't say anything. I don't think he's who they're looking for. If you do hear from him, tell him to lay low 'til this blows over. The way these things go, being an outsider and all, they'll turn him inside out before they're satisfied he's not who they're after."

"Thanks Jimmy," she said smiling at me.

"Get some rest, OK. And go easy on Peggy, she's just worried, that's all. You know she thinks the world of you," I said. She put her arms around me for the first time ever which made me worry that she might really be in trouble. Maybe she was shook up a bit. She was ice cold.

"You always gonna look after me, Jimmy?" she whispered. Somewhat curious, I nodded. We were never that close. An instant later she was gone.

I had a splitting headache by the end of the shift. It had crept up on me gradually, building up as I continued to work and flip the day's details over and over, trying to make sense of it all.

I wanted to further explore the spot where the odd UFO seemed to land but I went back in the direction of the apartment to rest first. I passed the spot on my bicycle but exhausted as I was and mindful of Didi's drama, I wasn't compelled to check it out. Approaching, I could see Tong sitting with his head buried in his hands on the two steps outside our building's front door. Upon seeing me, he got up and immediately went inside. I dropped my bike, followed and called after him. I heard his feet on the stairs then his door slam shut. I considered going upstairs and knocking but I already had too many things on my mind.

After a shower, a hot Cup'O Noodles and a nap, I dressed and considered going back out.

It was just after 6PM when I'd pedaled to the spot where I saw the strange orb. With all that's going on I felt a bit foolish. I never saw an alien vessel or their reputedly big headed green occupants, but it was weird and this was a weird week.

I come from a small town. In my experience, almost everything in a tiny system is related. My father had killed the wrong man but it turned out to be the right man's brother. This horrible little cluster of highway, concrete and woodsy glades was an even smaller system. All that happens, happens as expected when everyone who is here or passes through, acts as expected. If I call in sick, Doug is forced to stay late or come in early. Burke the Jerk never complained or sent back food when Doug was working and had to get his asshole fix satisfied somewhere else.

If a customer tries to skip out on the check, Doug chases him with an old Louisville Slugger whereas I would copy his plate number and put a call in to Barry Tiltson.

If everything was somehow related to the drifter, from the UFO to the dead animals, Didi's illness and the Amish murder, then it made sense to look at everything. If anything, it would at least give me something to talk about the next time I saw my old man, give him something to think about other than his predicament.

In the remaining sunlight, I stashed my bike where I could find it and wandered into the woods where the orb had gone. Maybe it was a fallen weather satellite, a big aluminum ballon. I could sell it on the internet or maybe collect a reward.

There was a relatively sharp declination which let me know I was getting close to the expressway. I made my way to the ridge and peered around at the thick brush and runaway thatches of weeds.

There was a dark spot. As I approached, I could see the surrounding greenery had been stomped flat. There was a space beneath a half dead tree.

It had been hit by lightning but refused to die completely or fall. What was left of the tree leaned over at such an angle that its massive roots had ripped through the ridge leaving a shallow slanting ditch shaded by their stiff and useless grasping tendrils.

There was something crunchy underfoot. I stopped to check it out. There had been a spill of something. Tip toeing around. I noticed a few other dried reddish puddles. I didn't think it was blood, blood didn't crystalize, not to my knowledge anyway.

Nearby, there was a swarm of flies on a small furry carcass. I took a last look around and a deep breath then stooped to go inside the ditch. After two steps in darkness, I felt metal underneath. I bent over to inspect it. I found the edge in the dirt, It was smooth and rounded. I guessed it was an old road sign but couldn't be sure in the dark. I searched around to get an idea of how far back it went and found a metal rod about three feet long. It was hollow and pointy at one end. The pointy end was sticky. My foot had found something soft, a knapsack. It was heavy, my heart started to pound. I was certain someone was using this little cave and could show up any moment. Nervously, I worked the zipper and stuck my hand inside the bag. I wanted to drag it out into the light but didn't want to be seen in case the owner was nearby.

There were magazines, clothing and some tangled wires. At the bottom, sleek plastic and metal cased gadgets, maybe a cell phone and other personal electronics. I wondered if it could be the Drifter's lair. If it was, the bag was full of things he certainly hadn't lifted from the Amish. I backed out and looked around. There was no one anywhere to be seen.

I ducked back in and dragged out the bag to check if there was any identification inside. In a zippered compartment were were dozens of business cards from eastern cities and an old Greek passport. It was the Drifter's. Dion was Dionysis Strobos.

Hastily, I put everything back and made my way to the spot where my bicycle was before it got too dark.

Pedaling back to the complex, I considered what I knew. It was insignificant despite how it felt. There was no gun, or stash of designer drugs as far as I could tell. I wasn't certain but I don't think there was anything illegal about living in the woods like an animal, unless of course he was eating people, which probably wasn't the case. I could call Tiltson and give him the Drifter's name, he could run it and see what came up.

I didn't really like the idea. I couldn't say that he'd done anything wrong. Other than possibly taking advantage of a young woman and even that seemed a stretch. Didi was 23, a city girl, ex-con and anything but naive.

I went home to see if anything could be learned about the Amish case on the news. There was a puddle in the middle of my bathroom floor and more water coming from the ceiling above. I ran upstairs to Tong's and banged on his door. There was no answer. I banged some more and yelled. Still there was no response then I recalled we had each other's keys in case of emergency and this seemed like an emergency. I went down and got them. I opened his door and called out then went to his bathroom which was right above mine. Water was flowing out of the tub he was lying in.

"Hey, wake the fuck up! You're destroying the place!" I didn't want to get too close to see anything awful. His head and shoulders were up against the side of the tub above the water but I couldn't tell if he was breathing or not. There was no blood in the water spilling out over the side like in the movies. I grabbed a towel, threw it over him and turned off the water. I touched his forehead, it was warm but so was the water. With a hand over his mouth, I found his breath and caught a heavy whiff of alcohol. I pulled the stopper. There was an empty glass on the floor but no pill bottles. No pills anywhere in fact. In the kitchen, I found a few empty green bottles of something called Soju.

Back in the tub, Tong had shifted a bit as the water was almost gone. I called the diesel station and told them that Tong would miss his shift, thereby upsetting our little ecosystem then went downstairs to clean up the mess.

When I rolled up to the lot at work there were police cars again, state troopers. They had Doug in the backseat where one of the troopers was questioning him. He looked pissed off. When they saw me, the cruiser's door opened.

"James Blindbear," The trooper called after me. I back pedaled and turned around.

"We've got some questions for you," he stated.

"Can we go inside. I need to get ready for my shift," I said politely.

"Suit yourself," he said.

Peggy was at the window watching. She followed me back.

"They're asking questions about Barry. He *never* went home last night," she told me.

"What about Didi?" I asked as the bathroom door burst open and Didi stepped out.

"I'm fine. They talked to me already."

She went out front to wait on a guy who just came in. She looked better, not just better than when last I'd seen her but better than ever. She was radiant, swift and graceful.

The trooper and I sat down, I watched him pull out his book and pen.

"James Sean Blindbear. You live here on the complex in apt 1B?" he asked

"For about three years now."

"When was the last time you saw Deputy Tiltson?"

"Yesterday around this time. We spoke about the investigation, you know, the thing with the Amish. I watched him leave. He got into his cruiser and left with Didi for Leola."

"Yes, we have that, we just spoke to Miss Jones. Did Barry say anything unusual or indicate there was something unusual about the case or mention something troubling him?"

"Other than the troubling aspects of the case itself, no. He was as normal as could be expected with everything going on," I said thinking about those moments; Barry waving at Peggy and lighting a cigarette as he walked to his car. I couldn't believe Old Barry would disappear in the middle of something, or even if he wasn't in the middle of something.

"What was your relationship to Deputy Tiltson?" he asked.

"Relationship?" I responded curiously.

"It's procedure. They all say you know Barry," he clarified.

"We all know Barry and he knows us. He looked me up about three years ago after doing my criminal history check to get this swell job," I explained indicating the greasy grill behind me.

"I don't have a common last name. He claims to have known my grandparents. Ever since, he stops in to shoot the shit a couple of times a month or so. He drives by to check in on the late shifts if he's in the area."

"Do you know if he had any enemies, or if someone had been holding a grudge?"

"Is that why you have Doug out in the cruiser?" I asked.

"Douglas Tibits has a record several pages long. His last interaction with law enforcement was Tiltson. A number of tickets, an appearance and a fine related to the state helmet law. Before that it was armed robbery and assault," the Trooper read to me.

"Well, we're not saints or senators out here frying eggs in hell. And Doug knows Barry was trying to keep him from cracking his head on the blacktop." I stood slowly looking over the trooper's head. The

Drifter was outside in the predawn darkness looking in. The trooper turned.

"Who's that?" he asked. Upon hearing this, Peggy turned to the plate glass and screamed when she saw him out there.

"It's him! He's your man, goddamnit!" she shrieked pointing an accusatory finger.

Seeing her, he disappeared in a blur. The trooper and I pursued but we both stopped dead in our tracks after we got out into the lot. There was no sign of him fleeing in any direction. The other trooper got out of his cruiser and looked at us curiously as his partner called out.

"Bobby, did you see anyone just now come running by?"

"No sir, but it's dark still and I was finishing up with Tibits here," he answered his fellow officer as Doug slowly got out of the cruiser himself to have a look around.

"That was Dionysis Strobos. He has a Greek passport," I told them.

"How do you spell it?" the trooper asked and I recited it as best as I could from memory. "That was the suspect Barry was after, the so called Drifter?" asked the trooper who had been speaking with Doug.

"Yes," I said regretfully, resigned to the idea that he was quite possibly the crazed sicko they were looking for.

"Where's he staying?"

"A ditch in the glade off the expressway. I found it earlier this evening but I didn't really know what to make of him 'til now," I explained.

"Bobby," he directed the younger trooper, "Recall the other unit and put in a call for one more. We may have a genuine man hunt on our hands this morning. Now, do you mind showing us where you found this ditch, Mr. Blindbear?" he said obviously enjoying the sound of my name way too much.

"Doug, can you cover me for and hour or so?" I asked as he was lingering. A truck had just pulled into the lot.

"You got it, Jimmy," he said. I could tell he didn't mind sticking around to see what came of everything. I hopped into the squad car and lead them to the half dead tree. The other car returned and I could see it slowly driving up and down the nearest section of glade, probing the dark woods with its searchlight.

Gun drawn, the trooper handed me his flashlight as we hovered over the ditch. "Aim it in there," he prompted and stepped past.

"Come out with your hands in the air!" the officer demanded. I ducked into the small space and held the flashlight high to illuminate as much of it as possible.

"It's not all that deep, just four or five feet beyond the dip," I told him. He went in and took two steps, disappeared. I heard a gunshot then an agonizing sob. I fought the impulse to flee, got close to the ground and searched with the light. I found him face down in a shallow grave like hole.

Leaning on its edge against the wall beside him was a the narrow road sign I'd stepped on earlier.

"Damn it, I think I broke my wrist. I fell on my hand holding the gun," he explained shamefully. I panned around in the small cave. The knapsack was gone. There were some small pieces of speckled egg shell from wild local birds scattered about.

The trooper stood up in the hole which seemed about three to four feet deep. He used his radio to call for a medic. There was a dirty blanket at his feet.

"Help me up, will you?" he asked and I did. We made our way back to the cruiser, the officer holding his gun and swollen hand as one. He couldn't drive. When he tried to raise his partner on the radio there was no response. Then he called for an EMT. I drove the squad car back toward the KwikiTrak.

In the darkness on the other side of the parking lot, a search light could be seen stabbing into the woods. We rushed to it. Not far from the vehicle, amongst the brush and wild weeds, was the other officer on his back. I aimed the cruiser's search light at him. Sticking out of his chest was a metal tube, his blood weakly pulsing out. It reminded me of the length of metal I had found in the cave just before dusk the other day. He must have been stabbed directly and deliberately in or near the heart, I thought seeing his blood pumping out into the dark air.

"Jesus Christ! What the fuck is happening here?" The state trooper dropped to his knees beside his co-worker. "He's still alive. Unconscious but living. Where's the fucking back up and the medics," he sobbed loudly while rocking back and forth holding his damaged hand.

From deeper in the woods, I heard the sounds of a struggle. I took the trooper's flashlight and scanned around in the darkness. There was something reflective. It turned out to be a fancy sneaker with a reflective panel in the thick white rubber heel. It had to be Didi's. No one else around here wore expensive sneakers.

I bound into the dark glade in the direction of the scuffle. Fanning the light ahead of me, I caught a glimpse of her being dragged by the ankle.

"Hey!" I yelled and regretted it immediately. If I didn't have the element of surprise, at least he may have mistaken me for the law if I'd kept my mouth shut. Hurrying along and trying to keep sign of them in my sight, I was stunned to be sideswiped and momentarily blinded. It was the orb up close, a brilliant greenish white metallic sphere about 7 feet wide. It floated like it had almost no weight and only knocked me down because it was shocking.

It could have been something inflatable, yet it seemed to move with alert purposefulness. I looked around and it was gone again.

I heard Didi call my name. She evidently recognized my voice when I called out or saw me scrambling after them with a flashlight. I continued on in what I hoped was the right direction, still trying to blink away the afterimage of the orb.

Getting closer to the end of the glade, I could hear trucks passing nearby. In the dim distant streetlight, I could make out the ridge and the grassy drop to the interstate.

The Drifter was nearby, his knapsack on his back and a large curving blade in his hand. Didi was flat on the ground twisting under his foot, her hands cuffed out in front, over her head. He saw my face in the twilight, a moment of eye contact. His expression didn't change at all. He raised the blade apparently aiming to behead her right in front of me.

I aimed the light in his face just as I sensed the swing. There was the dull sound of the blade striking earth. I charged and tossed the heavy flashlight at him. I missed. There was a streak of black and chrome. I made contact with someone and ended up on my back again. I found the blade buried a few inches in the ground and freed it. In another moment there was light in my face.

"Get up," the Drifter demanded without much enthusiasm. "I am certain you will always remember this day, what you have done here, what you set free. You will hear of her and know she his yours. I will not go after her. She will get stronger and stronger." He handed me the flashlight.

"Where's Didi?" I asked, still holding on to the blade even though I sensed he was meaning we should trade. Turning the light on him I could see blood on his neck and shoulder. It looked like a wild animal had just taken a swipe at him. His eyes were creepily bloodshot, the whites practically crimson. He smiled and turned away calmly. I could hear sirens approaching.

"What have you done?" I demanded.

"I have merely peeked into Pandora's box. You've lost the lid." He continued to make his way back through the woods towards the other side of the parking lot where I left the troopers.

"There are cops out there you know!" I called after him.

"Yes, and they definitely will want to talk with you," he said.

"You can't go around like this. People are dead,"

"I am only responsible for half of that," he said. Headlights were stabbing into the glade, car doors opening and closing loudly.

"What the hell is this about?" I asked still confused by it all.

"It's nearly daybreak. I haven't the time," he said. I heard Doug's Harley roaring furiously away in the distance. About to say something, I stopped realizing I was alone. I searched for a few moments to no avail and called out only to be answered by the trooper having his hand bandaged up by the EMT.

I dropped the blade and skirted the scene in the sparse cover of wild brush and ragged pines. I didn't want to see the trooper with the big metal straw sticking out of his heart or talk to any of the others without having a few moment to think.

It was after 6 AM when I walked back to the KwikiTrack Grill. Peg and Doug were outside, Doug pacing angrily back and forth. "I thought you were gone," I said confused at finding him. He continued pacing, hair flapping around his head. Peggy dropped her cigarette and stared off into the distance, into the darkness away from the pinkish glow swelling on the horizon.

"It's Didi. She came in a few minute ago like greased lightning. She knocked Doug on his ass and took his helmet," she said flatly.

"And my fucking bike, man. The bitch is on my fucking bike!" Doug added shaking with rage.

Just then, Burke the Jerk stepped out from the restaurant and opened his big mouth.

"Which one of you pussies is gonna fix my eggs?"

*General,*

*I include James Blindbear's early encounter with Strobos as it seems Strobos might have had the use of a very sophisticated drone. A drone's use might be indicative of accomplices with the kind of budget to facilitate the theatrics used to sway or bewilder his victims.*

*Blindbear was also entangled by one of Strobos's victims; Didi Jones. She is a dangerous and wanted fugitive who fled the scene of two Pennsylvania homicides. If she can be apprehended she may lead us to Strobos. I am only beginning to piece together her further involvement with evidence collected from Blindbear who is in custody currently. James Blindbear was arrested a couple of years for stalking a model whom he claims is Didi Jones. His blood toxicology report came back negative. He did however, have abnormally high levels of testosterone and HGH (Human Growth Hormone)*

*SSgt. F. Chandrastakar*
*Division of Forensic Studies*

# 3

**THE EDGES WERE SOFT...**

## 2005

I knew I had fired on him more than once. There was no longer a rational explanation for anything. The wet streets below gleamed with city light and my muscles ached from holding on to the windowsill. Looking away from the horrible scene inside the apartment and finding the not too distant neon sprawl of Time's Square so beautiful, I kept it in my sight in case it was to be the last thing I saw. I knew I couldn't hold on much longer and my other arm was numb.

I don't know exactly how I'd been disarmed, it was so fast. I'd warned him but he ignored me and pushed his victim to the floor so I fired and that got his attention.

When he turned to me, I froze. The whites of his eyes were scarlet. I fired again. There was more than just a muzzle flash. I saw his eyes but he seemed to be gone a moment.

There was a cold feeling in my shoulder and upper arm, his hand on the gun, then the gun was gone.

There was a burst of something on my radio demanding a response but there was nothing I could do, my other arm had become useless. Sweat burned and blurred my eyes. I kept blinking to clear them, to stay fixed on the life represented by the myriad of lights just blocks away.

It was understood that police work involved risks and I had taken a few in my four years of duty.

It was less than a week ago when Holly Zimmerman showed up at the precinct to try to find out how to get an order of protection against a guy she'd met online.

Normally, people came and went from the precinct house without notice unless they were notably insane or memorably attractive. Ms. Zimmerman had been quite attractive so I took notice. Her story seemed insane so I didn't forget it. I never met a woman who put an ad in the personal section of any paper or used an online dating service. If they had, they never owned up to it. Ms. Zimmerman hadn't been the type I expected. I couldn't understand why she'd have any trouble meeting men who were interested in her. I had held the belief that the kind of women using those services were obese, neurotic or had a STD.

When realizing she didn't have enough information about the creep to start the ball rolling, she settled for filing a report. That was when my nutcase alarm had gone off. She told us she met a young man who'd answered her ad. They'd met for coffee and then went to see live music at the Knitting Factory in TriBeCa. I have to admit I was a bit jealous and that jealously, as it occurred to me, is exactly what put me on this ledge today.

I knew by her shoes and handbag that she never dated civil servants. Ms. Zimmerman appeared to belong to the hip clique of lower Manhattanites who worked freelance from time to time between club hopping and jet setting, commonly found in cafes sitting behind sleek expensive laptops or tablets.

They were always subsidized by daddy, if not theirs someone else's.

The crazy part of her story which had my coworkers giggling and shaking their heads at me as I had followed her out starry eyed and practically tripping over myself, replayed in my mind.

She had referred to the guy as an eccentric and cautious man, quiet and well mannered. She had invited this weirdo up to her place after a second date. They'd gone to a photo exhibit in the West Village. Ms. Zimmerman knew the artist and wanted to show the man she called Donny Strobos an original print she had been given a few years ago.

The perp had brought her a bottle of wine and a tiny box of chocolate truffles. He'd dropped a glass and she stepped on a shard, cutting her foot. She told us how she'd panicked seeing all the blood but her new friend was calm and helpful, knew how to relax her.

He'd slowed and stopped her bleeding, had treated her like a princess then jumped out of her eighth floor window, the very one I dangled from.

Before she could cross the room with her bandaged foot, he knocked on her door.

I figured he'd drugged her and maybe her blood loss enhanced the drug's effect. It didn't matter much, whatever the problem was, I was ready to be her white knight. I'd given her one of the cards from the investigative unit with my name and badge number hastily scribbled in. I recommended a drug test but she had practically sneered at me for insinuating she could have been too stoned to know what had happened to her. I didn't let that discourage me. Romance always started with a little conflict, disagreements or petty bickering. At least that's how it worked in the movies. I didn't expect her to call the next evening.

She had the small box that the chocolates had come in and thought I could get prints off it.

The box had a texture which prevented the collection of a full fingerprint but it was not a common brand. They were Varda; a foreign chocolatier I had never heard of and couldn't afford to give to casual acquaintances like he had.

I went to their SoHo boutique and interviewed the fag who worked there hoping he'd remember a quiet, eccentric fellow.

He described the man Ms. Zimmerman had called Donny Strobos to my satisfaction but it only confirmed what I'd already known.

The candy retailer had nothing truly notable to tell me, only that the quiet eccentric man refused to taste any samples but smelled each and could recite with amazing accuracy each truffle's flavor, regardless of how exotic or rare.

There was noise coming from the apartment, a power tool. He was using an electric saw to cut Ms. Zimmerman's body up, starting with the head. Clearly, he could see my arm, shoulder and face over the windowsill. I didn't know what to do. He could saw my good arm off in a moment.

Riskily swinging my legs up to the windowsill, I tried to get back in but I couldn't maneuver it, couldn't get my foot in because the window wasn't wide enough.

For a fleeting moment, I considered letting go, freeing myself from the horror then I heard the saw stop.

"You'll never get away if you don't leave now!" I yelled hoping he would flee the scene without killing me. There was noting I could do for his victim now. He gently put Ms. Zimmerman's head in a plastic shopping bag.

"You sick, sick fucking bastard," I called him, almost sobbing after seeing the dead expression on her face. Whites of his eyes still blazing red, he looked at me dangling then closed them for a moment.

This beast, this butcher came towards me with a deliberate slowness, I could see the power to do the ungodly gather and bristle in his limbs. A colder sweat stung at my back in the wind as my body amped itself up for impossible flight.

A jump from this height could be fatal, I didn't want to be mutilated then fall.

He must have done this before, savoring my terror, my fear, my helplessness. Conveying with mere motion the awful magnificence of his being and ability, the saw in his hand seemed so much less significant.

"You don't know what it is, that I am. Blinding cycles wheel through time, spokes unaware of eternity's destination," he said and dropped the saw as he stood over me. "I shot you," I spoke aloud to a universe which stopped behaving in a manner I understood.

"It will take me hours to recover, days if I actually want to remove your shot," he responded rubbing a spot corresponding to a new hole in his vest. I could see he only wore a dingy white T shirt underneath. There was no body armor, no stiff Kevlar.

It seemed he wasn't in a rush to kill again. There was no way to tell how these crazies would act and I was still bewildered, curious.

"Strobos," I said and he fixed his gaze upon me directly.

"You've scene this face, you know my name. You must know her," he said indicating the mess on the rug.

"Why are you doing this?" I asked, my entire body trembling with the exertion. I couldn't hold on much longer.

"She never mentioned a policeman," he said.

"She doesn't really know me. She filed a report. We all know about you," I lied.

"Do you? They only sent you?" he asked incredulously.

"I was concerned," I said weakly.

"She was already dead. She would have become death itself," Strobos said.

"Help me, you Fuck! Help me!" I pleaded. He smiled and I was certain that he'd watch me plummet to the street below.

"You will accept help from me, the monster in your eyes. You see within me the capacity to save even though..." Before he could finish, I finally lost my hold. In an instant his hands clasped my head, tightening on my skull and I reached out to get hold of his arm. With what seemed like casual effort, he held me there above my death.

"It's muscle and flesh that keeps you in one piece. What do you know of peace, contentedness, true and absolute joy?" he asked.

"Not a lot," I said straining to move my mouth against his grip.

"To have some grasp of the endlessness yet only moments. I've never been envious of life," he said. My other arm recovered enough to reach for him when he suddenly leapt forward and out to fall with me. When he let me go I lost control of my bladder, flailed and grasped in empty air.

And it seemed the seconds ached past slowly. Once I caught sight of Strobos, I ignored my certain fate. He seemed to be deliberately moving through the air beside me, legs crossed in a lotus position like a floating monk or magic carpet riding jinn. Aware of my attention, he executed swift spirals around me. There was an inhuman shriek, a swerving delivery truck, my limbs being yanked painfully fast from the space my body occupied in the universe and then blackness.

The soothing smell of fresh baked bread was all around then there was a jolting stop and loaves wrapped in paper fell on me. Cool air above, I saw the top of the truck had been ripped open roughly and wide.

Miraculously, I was unharmed and not alone. I could hear the wrappers crinkling near me in the dark. The truck's driver came around the back to investigate. When he opened the doors, Strobos leapt out screaming and beat the man with French loaves, scaring him off.

I got up, took the radio handset off my belt and went outside to investigate. Almost reflexively, my thumb pressed talk but I had no idea where to start. In another moment, Strobos strolled up to me and I froze.

"The bread smells so good, doesn't it?" he said extending a loaf to me. There was a burst of static and unintelligible prompts from another unit.

"Go ahead. Use your radio. It's all marvelous now. We can both saunter. This was the only way." He turned away, casually strode to the middle of the street then streaked skyward. I remember staring at the radio for what seemed like an eternity, unable to make out anything said to me.

My shoulder was feeling better, residual pins and needles all the way to the fingertips.

Guiltily, I took a bite out of a loaf as I recalled Ms. Zimmerman's mutilated remains in the building above.

It was a year or so ago and the orderlies at the institution where I have to stay never get tired of hearing the story. I don't think they believe me anymore than my coworkers or the jury or the judge did, they were just kinder. The food and medication isn't too bad, I only wish there was a cute nurse somewhere in the facility.

There were games and crafts. I became good at puzzles, even the old ones whose pieces were not in good condition. The edges were soft and a little shapeless, difficult to fit together.

Sometimes, after they give me my meds, I lay awake drooling on myself, staring at spots made on the walls and ceiling by others. I recall reverent tone that Strobos imbued in the three syllables that made up the word *endlessness* and I whisper it to myself over and over, hoping to find my way to a dreamless sleep.

# 4

# "BLOODNURSE"

## 2016

It's no lie. Most of the creative types I come across are flaky pricks and this one had been no different. Sure, as a musician and composer myself, I'm a type of artist too but always fell short when it came down to leading the lifestyle. I didn't put sex and drugs and rock n' roll before everything and everyone else in my life. I had been a boy scout in my youth and when it came right down to it, I still took my merit badges quite seriously.

I liked a cup of tea in the early evening while enjoying nature shows on my curved 80 inch HD screen. I would sit on the sofa, cozy in my thickest velour robe, watching river slickened black grizzlies pealing live salmon to devour their fatty skins, or Indian elephant newborns making their first appearance from the womb in jungle mud. Some evenings, I liked to mull wine and have guests over for drinks and a hike. We'd discuss art and music while pausing at magnificent boughs and broad trunks out in the crisp woods nearby which were often fragrant with chimney smoke.

The prick of the month had been Devon Trang, a half Thai Chinese MIDI prodigy from California who had flown to Boston then came up to my place in Plymouth this Fall. After adding some custom effects to a group of resampled .wav files I made of his MIDI work, I looped them and put them back into the mix of his new solo demo.

After previewing the recordings, he'd joined me for tea and watched the nature shows. He had two cups and used up the last of my organic honey.

Trang smoked some hashish while gazelles fornicated on the vast Serengeti, then masturbated a bit too loudly in the upstairs bathroom.

He wore his hair dreadlocked and preferred to walk about shoe and shirtless. I was sure he had been one of the jerks who was good at hacky-sack when it was popular.

His cell phone rang incessantly, a different ring tone for each of the young women he was stringing along after the last tour. I honestly didn't have anything against him personally until now. We were just two different ends to the same story.

We were flying down to Florida to meet the executive producer and his yes men in South Beach.

The tracks were late, which was Trang's fault but it was my project so I had to go with him to help smooth things over with the hotshots and assure them whatever input they have will be reflected in the final mixes.

It was South Beach because we were late to meet in Boston two weeks ago and had to catch up with them while they caught rays, sipped umbrella'd drinks enjoyed spa time. Trang wore jeans, sandals and a hand painted tank top even as it was late October. At the airport, he asked to borrow my blazer because he was cold and had packed his colorful trademark Himalayan hand knit cardigan away in the bag he checked.

After we got coffee and muffins at Starbuck's he must have warmed up a bit. He gave my jacket back and went to use the restroom. In the pocket, I found a sticky chunk of hashish wrapped partially in foil. It usually took more than drugs at an airport to freak me out but it was wrapped quite inseparably in aluminum foil. If I stuck it in his carryon bag it would be seen with X-rays just as easily as if I left it in my pocket.

Trang was nowhere in sight. Across the room was a large trash bin. I would lose my place in the cue to check in but at least I could deal with finding him and checking in without worrying about going to jail. I wondered how he planned to get past security with it or if he'd had a plan at all. I hated the idea that I might have been his plan.

As I stepped off the line to throw the sticky crap away, I froze at the sight of a uniformed man with a very professional looking dog at his side. I expect a drug and bomb sniffing dog to be on staff at an airport, although I have never seen one outside of the arrivals area.

This combined with the missing prick was going to send me into space. I stood in the line while making frantic calls to Trang's cell phone to no avail.

I considered dropping the chunk on the floor but the dog was really intimidating and the airport wasn't the best place to drop or leave anything unattended. Everything I knew from the Nature Channel about the sense of smell flashed in my mind. A bear's nose is reported to be 40 times as sensitive as a dogs but facts like those were of no use to me.

I had played with the little dark sticky chunk in my pocket. Perhaps I reeked of hash already. If odor was the result of the source's airborne molecules then the hash molecules should be all over me. Feeling too paranoid to just step from the line and toss it in the trash without arousing suspicion, I did the only thing seeming to make sense at the moment.

Unwrapped, I stuffed it deep into my chocolate walnut muffin and ate it. It seemed to be the sensible thing to do. I've only ever seen hash heads like Trang smoke it. Hashish is made from marijuana, the pressed material from the buds or flowers of the plant, I wasn't sure if it was heated or not, but I didn't believe so. It's a process known as decarboxylation. Without heat, a cannabis product was merely vegetable.

I took his bag and got off the line. There was still time. I went into the nearest restroom.

Hashish gone, sticky foil in the toilet, hands washed, I felt a bit foolish realizing I should have just tried to flush the whole thing.

A bit calmer, despite the feeling in my stomach, I looked for Devon Trang everywhere. I even staked out the nearest lady's room to see if he had somehow managed to hook up with a pathetic sycophant who wanted to get laid on her layover by a rising electro star.

Almost 40 minutes passed. It was getting close to the time when I was certain we'd miss the flight.

I considered going without Trang and wondered what I'd say to the people in South Beach.

Back in the queue to check in, I started to feel dizzy. With thoughts about vomiting, I went back into the men's room and watched in the mirror as my pupil's dilated. All of my muscles and joints felt new, smooth and more flexible than I could recall. Overcome with a moment of childish delight, I touched my toes a few times. I stretched and flexed muscles that really haven't been used for a while until some guy came in and caught me arching my vertebrae like a cat.

I started to feel good, started to giggle. It seemed my brain was floating blissfully out of my head until the colors, lights and announcements danced and became dreamlike, confusing.

Perhaps I went out for air. Maybe I ran into Devon Trang while he autographed a row of female fans on their tattooed and peach fuzzy tailbones with a silver Sharpie pen.

Maybe it wasn't him, maybe it was a sweaty Mexican with a flock of clucking birds or a Chinese parking attendant inventorying a rack of swinging denim giraffes...

Having lost track of reality, I became a hysterical pendulum swaying back and forth from joyous liberty to complete paranoia.

A cab driver pulled up and I must have proffered a form of international or trans-dimensional affirmative, because he took what was left of my luggage and opened the door for me. To sit and pull away from the airport afforded me a reprieve until I passed out and urinated on myself.

The cab driver clearly took exception to my state and dumped me somewhere along the road at dusk. The amber and scarlet in the brisk air made me feel like I was exploring Mars.

Away from the highway, I stumbled and rolled down rocky inclines and barren scratchy brush. For an unaccountable amount of time, I was lost in a dream or a flashback to a day in summer camp. I recalled the sticky paper cups of fruit drinks and splinters from old picnic furniture.

I began longing for a sleepy ride home. It was after dark when I became more aware of my situation. Still quite pleasantly high, I didn't panic. The world seemed more interesting on hashish, almost like it did with the fancy hydro hybrid kindbud passed around years ago when I weathered a stint in Los Angeles as a sound engineer.

I paused and leaned against big cool rocks and tried to take stock of the situation.

The temperature dropped then it started to rain. I stripped off my pants, spread them flat over some of the taller brush and hoped the rain would cleanse my little accident away before putting them back on. I had remote visions that bordered on hallucination, all involving man eating beasts which would would home in on human piss and dismay. I tried to take it seriously but couldn't.

Still stoned, my disposition wasn't bad even though I was drenched and would probably catch a cold. I searched for my cell phone but couldn't find it.

I took the pants and started to wring them out while looking around in the darkness for my next move. It had to be shelter and warmth. I needed time to recover somewhat. I needed for the rain to stop, for the sun to shine. I had to find my way back up to the highway.

Remotely, I knew there would be bad phone calls and strings of humiliating apologies. "Devon Trang. Devon Trang, Devon Trang!" I repeated the name over and over, the hash's magical mirth dissipating in the cold darkness of the hour. "Devon Trang," a voice weakly called out over the pitter patter of large raindrops in the surrounding trees. I stopped moving entirely.

Frightened, I repeated it. Again the voice came. I ducked and grabbed my pants, knotted the damp legs around my neck like a sweater then searched the darkness.

Again, I heard the prick's name, a female's voice. It seemed close. If I hadn't still been a little stoned, I probably would have fled.

Like I said earlier, the world was just a little more fascinating.

"Hello," I offered in the wet darkness.

"Help me. Over here, help me please," the woman's voice came again. I followed it along very big boulders and jagged formations below the sloping curve of highway above.

Almost hidden by the surrounding stone in the night, I could make out twisted chrome. There had been a car wreck. I approached carefully on hands and knees, feeling my way through the mud, ignoring creepy crawling things passing through my fingers and sticking to my shins.

"In here. Hurry," she said as I got close to the wreck. The car had crumpled and overturned. Only a slight recession in the rocky ground saved the passenger section from being crushed completely. I had to bite my tongue having almost remarked, "*You sure are lucky!*" Clearly, whoever was trapped in the wreck didn't consider themselves lucky, even as their rescue was finally becoming a possibility.

"I'm pinned behind the front seat, trapped," she whispered.

"I should probably go for help. I can't even see you. Are you alright? I mean, I know you are not alright, but can you last a little longer? Are you seriously hurt?" I asked, feeling a bit foolish.

"Don't leave me," she pleaded in the dark.

"Well, what can I do?"

"Get me out of here now," she demanded. I leaned in as close as possible to try getting a look. She must have been able to see me because I could hear her moving.

"It's raining pretty hard out here," I said nervously.

"Are you alone?" she asked.

"Yeah...It's complicated," I told her, images and worries of the day receding into a vague distance.

"Give me your hand," the woman asked. There was a moment when I had an instinct to turn around and get as far from her as I could, but thought it was just cannabis paranoia.

Slowly, I extended my hand and almost jumped when the shaky, cold and bony thing grasped my fingers. She guided me to the vinyl I easily recognized as the smooth expanse of the front bench found in many late model cars.

"Pull here. Pull with all your might," she told me. I squirmed closer to get a better grip and some leverage then pulled for what seemed a small eternity before feeling something give way.

"Are you OK?" I asked.

"I'm good now but I think you'll have to carry me. I feel weak and I'm hungry," she said. What was left of her clothing was coming apart in my hands. She was practically skin and bone. Her size and weight seemed impossibly small or I was still stoned and feeling like a superbeing.

"How long have you been out here?" I whispered as I gathered her high in my arms and stepped back into the rain.

"Long enough."

"Weeks?" I suggested.

"Longer."

"Jesus," I said quietly, trying to imagine the hell of wasting away alone out here in this nightmare.

"There are small hollows in the jagged rocks. Animal's hide in them," she told me.

"How do you know? Hey, I'm sorry. I forgot to ask. Were you alone in the car when the accident happened?" I questioned her, pausing in the darkness. Still the boy scout.

"Yes," she informed me.

"What's your name? I'm Colin Quade."

"Friends call me Drew."

"Nice to meet you, Drew. After it lets up a bit and we get you settled, I'm going back up to the road to flag someone down, get help," I told her, trying my best to sound confident.

"No, don't leave me here after all this."

"Well, what can I do? You clearly need medical attention. I don't think it would be safe to make the climb while carrying you. It seems easy now only because we are going down hill a bit."

"You're bleeding," she stated.

"Yeah, I got s few scrapes on the way down."

"I could smell it on you, your blood."

"You really have been out here far too long," I said recalling an instant when I had considered putting my hashish lined jacket on Trang's bag and telling the officer with the trained dog the jacket and bag's owner was in the can and neglectfully left them unattended. I imagined Trang was probably up in the sky, enjoying the inflight movie, the tiny vodkas, trying to get into the Mile High Club with an air hostess.

"So you can...uh, smell blood?" I asked in my most civilized conversational tone.

"Yes, it's a survival technique honed in despair and isolation."

"Oh," I carried her in to a low crevice in the jagged rock. Out of the rain at last. It was dank and irregular. I hoped not to twist my ankle on the uneven ground to avoid dying with the unfortunate and somewhat crazed crash victim.

"I'm so thirsty," she whispered in the darkness.

"I'm sorry. I don't have anything. I'm here by accident as well," I told her.

"Are you alright? What about your wounds?" she asked

"Never mind me, I'll be fine. I don't feel anything too serious. You're the one who needs real medical attention," I reminded her.

"My injuries are old. I no longer bleed. Let me clean your wounds. You saved my...life. It's the least I could do considering your kindness."

"Oh no, that's alright. Totally unnecessary. I was down here anyway, had a bit of time on my hands."

The next thing I know, she grasped my ankles and then I felt a rough little tongue on my leg.

"You really shouldn't be doing this. I need a bath for one thing."

I tried to jerk my leg away but her grasp on me was suddenly quite firm. It was weird, gross and creepy as hell, but I also pitied the poor creature as she cleansed my cuts and scrapes with her mouth. I really should have put my pants back on some point earlier, I thought, realizing they were still stuck to my back like a wet cape.

"This is to keep infection away," she explained, "like when you have a snake bite."

"Yeah, I've heard something like that," I said sitting down, resigned to my fate as her companion of sorts for the time being.

Mind blank in darkness, the insanity went on. She found the gash in my thigh. When I actually felt her tongue in the wound, I could not recognize the sound that came out of me.

A few minutes later, she spoke to me as if nothing peculiar had transpired at all. It went beyond that even, giving me the feeling we had been following a routine for the better part of the century.

She wanted me to block off our little grotto's entrance to keep her safe while I hunted. As absurd an idea as it seemed, I did as I was told.

I slipped into a mode of placating behavior; my coping skill set developed while working with pop divas and other pompous creative types.

Somehow, in the first fifteen minutes of our interaction, the frail, crazed and isolated woman evoked my masochistic side, which was at the very foundation of my abilities when it came down to handling the neurotic prima donnas cultivated by the music industry.

The hunting was another issue altogether. It implied belief and a certainty that we would stay in that hole for an extended period, which didn't suit me at all. Beyond that, despite my enthusiasm for the Nature Channel and the countless predators I've watched take down their prey, bigger and sharper than life on my OLED TV, I wasn't ready to kill, skin or gut anything.

As a boy scout, I learned how to clean a fish but never really got comfortable with viciously manipulating or mutilating anything as it flopped around in what was surely horror, pain and mortal fear. Ask me to build a solar powered pond water distillery, make a compass from a safety pin or start a fire without matches and I'm your man.

I found part of a fender nearby, perhaps from her wreck, perhaps another. In her trunk was a rough wool blanket and some old newspapers. There was a plastic flashlight that didn't work and a tire iron I salvaged as a weapon.

After closing off as much of the small hollow's entrance while making certain we weren't trapped, I decided to rest. With hope for a better tomorrow, I had slept dreaming of the special hush and comfort of air travel. There was no way to know how long I rested. Jolted into wakefulness by a distressful noise, the body's fight or flight response was in full swing. There was a long creaking wail in the darkness, a pitiful animal sound.

"What the fuck is going on?" I clung to a slimy wall hoping not to be mauled by whatever wild creature had gotten past my barrier. The scream became shrill and then dropped off suddenly.

"I got us food," Drew said.

"What?"

"A small animal came in. I have it," she said calmly. Then there was a slurping, sucking sound.

"What is it?" I asked, feeling a remote and primitive pang of hunger.

"A small mammal," she answered.

"Oh, good," I said, considering the alternatives.

"Do you want its haunches?" she asked as I heard a nauseating, flesh dampened cracking.

"Maybe I'll save it for morning. I could cook some if we could get a fire going."

"It really should be consumed. The blood will attract larger predators," she warned.

"I doubt it. We're only a few hundred yards from the highway," I said, "besides, the sun should be out soon, which is great because it's really starting to give me the creeps in here."

"I'm awake and feeling much better. I'll take care of you, *Baby*," she said, pain, fear and frailty gone from her voice.

"Just rest a little longer. Wait for your sun. I'll watch over you."

I only woke again because I couldn't toss and turn. When I tried and couldn't sit up, I thought it was a nightmare, the kind where you're lucid yet powerless to control your inert form.

When I recognized the feeling of her mouth on the wound in my thigh, I screamed. My hands and ankles were pinned intractably, almost inexplicably.

"Drew!" I hollered, almost unable to believe my assailant was the lost broken woman I'd carried in my arms. Trying to break free, it felt as if there were two sets of hands holding me.

There was the reek of death and burning flesh. Light stabbed across the tiny cave in fine mottled beams which managed to get by my make shift screen of found junk, but I couldn't really see anything.

"What the hell are you doing!"

She had opened up a cut on my leg and had her filthy mouth on it again. It seemed her feet curled grossly around my ankles like some kind of monkey foot. Again, I tried to shake her off me. I tried to put my knee in her face but she was too fast. I tried to reason with her.

"Listen, I know you've been through something dreadful, you've been out here for god knows how long. You don't have to do this. We are going to be OK. After you get some much needed professional attention, I'll take you out for a big brunch or lunch, whatever. We have definitely been through something together out here and I will not forget it or fail to recognize or downplay the significance of such a positive and life affirming experience this is for us both."

"I don't intent to harm you Mr. Quade. You have saved me already. I owe you more than you can comprehend," she said, "Now, I really need this of you. It will help me out much more than that animal's blood."

"I don't recall any survival technique involving the ingestion of human blood. I let that whole snakebite infection thing go earlier because I thought you were a little frazzled from being out here so long," I said. "I've been starving out here for *seventeen years*," she claimed gravely. Upon hearing this, I was certain she was insane from the accident. Her mind must have locked into a primitive survival mode. I'd heard of things like this on the Nature Channel. There were accounts of people lost in verdant forest glades for months. Many who survive suffer a type of post traumatic stress syndrome accompanied with a break in subjective reality, especially in the cases where a loved one is lost or a limb is severed.

In cases where civilized people have had to trap, hunt and kill to survive, life was never quite the same after they rejoined society. It seemed I've stumbled upon a prime example and would have to bear with her to a certain extent to help her through the ordeal.

I didn't believe the bit about seventeen years. I was absolutely certain the poor woman was delusional.

"This is going to hurt some Mr. Quade. I don't mean you harm, but it will hurt," she said as she braced me more firmly then opened a wound which was trying to scab over.

I don't know what people mean when they say a person has gone into shock, I've only heard it in films or read about it in newspapers. After the tearing of my flesh and feeling her loudly suck the life blood from my thigh, I knew a place beyond the pain. I began to feel a type of existential numbness.

The horrible sensation had overshot my pain threshold like a sound that had become too high in frequency to hear. I lost all sense of self. All thought processes shut down, the facilities of those processes absorbed solely by the visceral event.

I flashed back to the airport, felt the stickiness of the hashish still on my teeth. I considered the idea of still being under its effects. Was this a nightmare or was the life I could recall a dream?

My chattering teeth woke me hours later. There was a crackling fire in the cave. I rolled towards it, reawakening the throbbing wound in my leg and refreshing the horror of the earlier interaction which seemed a little unreal in the new warm comfort.

Just beyond the smoke, I started to make out a face. I was seeing her clearly for the first time. She moved closer to the flickering light after noticing I was awake. She smiled at me. Her face was attractive, younger than I expected, but there was a hardness to her sharply chiseled features which gave her an almost ferocious appearance not softened by her amicable expression.

"How do you feel this sundown?"she asked as if I had just woke from a peaceful afternoon's nap in my favorite comfy chair.

"Like shit. I feel weak," I said.

"You need to feed. You should have taken what I offered you last time," she said while poking the fire with the tire iron.

"We're going to die in here with all the smoke."

"No. I took down your barrier. Look. If you lean back you can see the stars," she said.

"Yes, very romantic. Well, this has been great, really. And a lovely little place you have here too. So...Anyway, I have some things to do, places to be, people to meet. You know. Promises to keep, miles to go before I sleep."

I lifted myself up carefully to try walking away from it all. Drew leaned forward and put an arm on my shoulder. Up close, without the veil of smoke, her face, although quite attractive was criss-crossed with dark veins and other blood vessels giving her skin an almost marbled appearance.

"I still need you Mr. Quade. Further, for being my blood nurse I will make you a gift of the oldest of living dreams. Dominion over time."

I stared at her for a few long moments. I wanted to scream, cry or slap her. I felt trapped in the situation.

It was no longer a matter of helping out an unfortunate accident victim, I was now dangling from a lunatic's fringe. I was hungry and felt dizzy. I had no idea how much of my blood had been spilled or consumed and I had to do something about it. She leaned over me, gently closed my eyes with her fingers and spoke softly, almost as if having read my thoughts.

"I heard a female owl's hoot not too far from here. I'll bet she has a nest, I really could use some fresh eggs and it would benefit you to eat as well." She kissed my forehead and stepped out into the night.

As soon as it was certain, by the surrounding silence, that she was far enough away, I got up and weakly carried myself out. The privacy of the moment allowed me the opportunity to relieve myself near a tree. My mind manufactured a mantra, I couldn't ignore, a familiar bit of childish alliteration; *curiosity killed the cat, curiosity killed the cat, curiosity killed the cat...*

I always liked a roaring fire. I don't know if my passion for the Nature Channel had anything to do with it, but I started to crave huge fresh owl eggs. I was starving. Besides, getting back to civilization would eventually entail embarrassing engagements with my current employers and even some pompous brow beating by that prick, Trang. Maybe just this once, all that could wait, and if Devon Trang's solo debut tanked, so be it.

In ten minutes, she was back. She had four small dark speckled eggs and what appeared to be a deep laceration in her forearm from the offended bird's talon.

"Good Christ, that looks painful. You need a poultice or something," I said, trying to getting into the spirit of things .

"That's nice but not necessary."

"Those eggs are quite a bit smaller than I had imagined. I hope it's worth the efforts," I said uncertain of who I pitied more, the fowl or the freak.

"It was almost as if she knew why I wanted them," Drew said, examining her arm. She sat by the fire across from me and skewered a pair of the small eggs on a twig she'd stripped green with her fingernails. She passed it to me and I held it over the fire as if they were the marshmallows or s'mores of my young scouting days.

Her face, serene in the fire's light, seemed so rational and intelligent. I couldn't bring myself to stomp off in a huff and demand what the hell was going on in her head. Her placid behavior made it feel socially wrong to act that way at the moment, besides, I was truly hungry.

Drew ate her eggs immediately, raw. When I saw her chewing, I realized they must have been fertilized and had live embryos inside. Smelling the fluid that dripped and sizzled into the fire from my egg kabob made me loose my appetite. She giggled at my dismay and picked a small fibrous strand of tissue from her teeth.

"Taste just like chicken," she joked then took the stick from me.

"I'll cook your eggs longer and save them for later. You'll eat eventually."

My stomach growling, I curled up in front of the fire and watched her cook in the primitive space.

At one instant, there was a fleeting yet familiar sent of fowl. My mouth watered. If only I could pretend it was a chicken wing. Suddenly, there were crazy shadows in the firelight, a cacophonous shriek and frantic flapping which broke the peace of our moment. I saw Drew move. A few seconds later there was only the sound of her breathing and the fire's low crackle. Then there was a gross and wet breaking sound. Hands covered in fresh frothy dark blood, she offered the dead owl's heart to me.

"Eat," she said, holding out the warm knot of muscle tissue a little smaller than a walnut.

"I've always been a leg and breast man myself. You're welcome to that," I told her backing away as she slurped up all the blood on her hands.

"In a week or so you'll crave this, we all do. This is not always so easy to come by. I'm practically spoiling you," she said and bit off a piece and savored it with near animal abandon. My stomach tried to turn inside out. She ate the rest and laughed watching me writhe and convulse with dry heaves.

"I'll cook you some of that big bird, but don't get used to it. Food as you know it, will soon be a part of your past," she informed me.

It was cold and damp, the desperate early hours of morning. The part of my mind that was awake or at least active had only been concerned with warmth and creature comfort. I was a shivering fetal lump inching closer to the dying embers.

The part of the mind involved with leading my life was in a far off escapist never land of vast green rolling meadows. I was an adolescent bounding towards the horizon amidst swaths of giant dandelion blooms trying to defeat gravity with a pair of big helium balloons lashed to my forearms.

Reality crept in, a thin gentle hand, the tender touch of a lover. She caressed my throat briefly then ran her fingers over my chest and shoulders. Fully awake, I froze and she pulled herself closer. She was as cold as stone which instinctively made me pull her to me to warm her up.

Snaking her other bony arm under my waist, she unzipped my fly. When her icy cold fingers played over my tightening scrotum, I didn't know which impulse to give in to.

Before there was time to think or decide, she whispered in my ear.

"I don't mean for this to hurt. If we were somewhere more convenient with the right mechanisms and pharmaceuticals... Well, we'll just have to make do." She bit into the soft muscle on my back between my shoulder blade and neck. The pain, sharp initially, was made abstract or seemed to attach it self to the sexual euphoria raising the intensity.

Carelessly adrift, I forgot everything until hearing the awful slurping of my blood. She only took what she called surface blood, or circulated blood to avoid breaking a blood vessel so I 'd heal up quickly for next time. To helplessly let life's substance flow away from the body was an unnatural thing, so much so, I couldn't help trying to squirm away.

"Take it easy, Lover. It just gets better from here," she whispered as reality ebbed away to the beat of my pumping heart.

It was early in the AM's again when I awoke. I could tell by the sparse and speedy traffic, mostly big rigs on long hauls in darkness.

With the sound of every gear and brake in the damp night air, I entertained an escapist segment in which my late father's truck would pull up and I would step into the cab and disappear. We'd be transported to the mid seventies on a Warm Summer Sunday afternoon and go out for waffles or French toast.

Finally on the road the next evening, I vomited in a filthy sink in a service station restroom that reeked of diesel and despair. Drew had fed me some salty gruel I feared was mostly animal blood but drank it just the same. I was starving and must have lost a lot of weight by the way my clothes hung, pants bunched up at the waist like a trash bag.

When she told me the warm mess I'd swallowed was mostly her own blood and tears, I knew I wouldn't be able to keep it down. I had been vomiting ever since, much more than expected. It was much more than I consumed, practically quarts of dark, chunky unidentifiable crap. I felt dizzy and weak. Her hero at one instant, I had become a wreck. She practically had to carry me. I washed my face and stepped outside.

There was a small van idling at the gas pump, its driver consulting the station's attendant inside under the greenest fluorescent tube I'd ever seen. As the men conversed, I saw Drew climb inside the vehicle. She slid open the cargo door and motioned for me to join her. I hesitated for a moment then caught a glimpse of something so feral in her eyes that a distinct fear of what she might do if I didn't follow, propelled me forward. I flopped down on a pile of smelly paint tarps and tried to make myself comfortable.

The van's driver came back with a hot cup of coffee and a folded road map. He was a paunchy looking fellow in his late forties, face tanned crimson from decades of working outdoors.

Drew swiveled in her bucket toward the driver's side door and smiled broadly at the man when he stepped in. His mouth hung open but no words came out initially. It was dark and Drew was female.

"Little lady, don't you know what kinda trouble you could get yourself into by climbing in folk's cars in the wee wee hours?" he asked smirking a bit. Obviously flustered, he tried to keep his cool while looking to see if anyone else was around. "My name is Drucilla. I thought a man like you could use a little company on the road, in these lonesome, wee wee hours." "Where might you be headed tonight?" he asked slowly as his heterosexual instincts shifted into gear. He closed the door and put it in drive.

"We're just going down the road a ways to be discrete," she purred coyly.

"I'm not exactly in the black as the high rollers say, but if you'll take forty, I'm all yours, Sweet thing," he said and licked his lips in lusty anticipation.

"How's about them trees up at the bend?" he suggested.

"That'll do me just fine," Drew answered quietly, grave notes in her voice easily be mistaken for provocation. The van pulled in tight near a pair of sagging dead pines, crunching cones and bristles as he parked.

"I heard about things like this but I must admit, I have never seen one of you gals up 'round here," he said spinning his seat to the back of the van where he saw me, presumably in the spot where he thought he was going to get laid. Nervous myself, I grinned.

"What in the fuck?" he yelped as Drew leapt upon him and smashed his head against the driver's side window hard enough to crack the glass. Petrified, I could only watch.

Drew or Drucilla, as she'd introduced herself moments ago, opened the door and dragged her prey to the ground. She threw the man's wallet back in at me. I could hear fabric tearing and then the unearthly thick slurping I had become all too familiar with. Remotely and quite oddly, I felt a tiny stab of jealousy.

Seeking distraction, I opened the wallet. The name on the license was Robert Jenks. He only had 28 dollars. I lifted myself up and felt queasy. Robert Jenks was a crumpled, convulsing heap against the side of his van, a sloppy diagonal crimson black gash dripping blood under his chin.

Drucilla stood over him in the darkness yet seemed to radiate a visible force, her image almost pulsing in and out of view. Exultant, she looked amazing, and knew it, her pride all the more obvious in my awestruck gaze. It was almost as if I was seeing her for the first time in the full flush of her youth and vitality. With one arm, she lifted Jenks and tossed him into the woods quite effortlessly. When the world was silent, all cicadas and distant traffic, she came back into the vehicle peacefully, despite the last few minutes of activity.

"You have his money?" she asked.

"Yeah, all twenty eight bucks," I said. She hopped back into the van and started to drive. I climbed into the passenger seat and took Jenks's coffee.

"Caffeine is not a good thing. You don't want to be restless after sunrise," she warned.

Drucilla drove with the reckless abandon of a big city cab driver. It was no wonder I found her in a wreck.

An hour or so later, we pulled into a small strip mall, its shops long closed. The rows of signs, lights and lettering seemed suddenly alien to me as if I'd arrived in a foreign country. Drew stepped out and looked back at me.

"I shouldn't be long. Are you coming or will you wait?" she asked. Feeling a bit odd, I climbed out slowly and followed. I was still weak and feeling nauseous.

Walking along the shuttered shops, Taco Bell, Game Stop and others, I felt somewhat out of place, above it all vaguely. I wondered if it was a feeling shared by fugitives, career criminals and homicidal maniacs. I was almost certain when the police caught up to us, I would be charged as an accomplice, or because of being a man, they might even think I was putting her up to the mayhem.

Drew walked up to the Marshall's and opened the locked door with a loud snap. Screws and tiny bits of metal bounced away in her wake as an alarm clanged loudly. "Over there!" she shouted, pointing to the luggage, "Get us a travel bag." She disappeared into a small room at the front. I unzipped a huge duffel and put it up on the sales counter as if we were ready to pay.

Drew stepped back into sight smiling as she waved a few neat bundles of new one dollar bills. She tossed them at me and I put them in the bag. In a few moments, she came back with an armful of clothing and stuffed it in as well. I grabbed a few pairs of sunglasses from a sales display.

We got back in the van and took off. She had me keep an eye out for motels close to the highway. It was an hour before we found one. Drew was quiet. Behind us, I could see the faint scarlet band of morning on the horizon.

"Go to the office and pay for a couple of nights, quickly." Duress in her voice obvious.

"Are you alright?" I asked, aware for the first time of my genuine concern since finding her in the wreck.

"That old prick must have been on a drug, some medication. I'm freezing," she said, beads of sweat rolling off her face which was crisscrossed with dark veins again.

"When you come back for the bag, bring me one of the blankets from the room. It's going to be close," she'd called after me as I walked away.

I stumbled into the management office causing the desk clerk to abruptly drop his book and reading glasses.

"You doing alright, Son?" he started and stood up further to assess my disposition. I must have looked like complete shit.

"We just need a room for a couple of nights, Gotta catch us some shut eye," I said feigning a bit of good natured regionalism.

"You and who else?" he asked.

"The uh...Misses, she's out in the lot. We got the heat on and she don't want us driving no further tonight," I explained. I must have reeked of sweat and vomit so I kept my distance as I counted out 129 dollars, mostly in crisp new singles.

Relieved that the man asked nothing else, I signed the book, took the key and went to the room. It was small but looked like a palace in comparison to the cave. I yanked the blanket off the bed and went back out to the van.

Drucilla had pulled up to the door. Daylight was spilling over the horizon like molten lava. Blanket stretched out in my arms, I wrapped her in it as she swiftly stepped out. I could feel her trembling almost violently. Even through the rough worn wool of the motel blanket, I could feel tremendous heat emanating from her body, impossible heat. Covered, she ran to the room in a trail of smoke reeking of singed flesh.

I was finally beginning to understand and accept the possibility I'd kept pushing away. Words formed in my head and I couldn't push them out. I grabbed the duffle and went into the room to find the shower running.

Drew was under the stream cooling off in a fetal coil, her bare lean back covered in fading Polynesian tattoos, sun welts on her arms and face. There was something so human and so pitiful about the fetal position. I couldn't help my eyes from tearing up.

Gently, I touched her shoulder and her hand curled over mine.

"Are you going to be okay?" I asked, now crouching beside the tub.

"I'm going to need you again tonight, while you're still halfway normal," she whispered, "and while you can still go out, get me a dozen eggs."

The sun was high in the sky as I made my way to the nearest convenience store. I purchased a dozen eggs and a squished loaf of Wonder bread. Despite the cool autumn air I was very warm, perspiring. My shirt stuck to my back and my eyes were tearing behind my stolen shades.

I had some idea how this was supposed to work from the horror films of my teen years. I'd drank Drucilla's blood and recalled the outrageous promise she'd made. I've witnessed some very convincing things. I saw her lob an unfortunate man into the woods, the terrible heat and sun welts on her body and the weird radiance that enveloped her upon drinking human blood. There was my own discomfort in daylight to consider. I didn't know if these things added up to truth, but I dared it to be true. I dared the entire universe to turn itself inside out for me and reveal everything that's ever been dreamed. I dared Drucilla to make the promise of everlasting life a reality.

I entertained the remote fear that I could possibly be in a holding cell somewhere, mind still spinning on a chunk of greasy black hash. Was drug time like dream time? Could this entire episode be a fantasy spun in a matter of minutes as I lay writhing on a filthy floor awaiting my current employer's attorneys?

I was independent, I was free of her for the time being, but wanted to see where this would go. If it was just in my mind, I may as well enjoy it. If it's real and I could become a form of eternal being, I wanted it to carry on. If I turned out to be the drug addled accomplice to a crazed serial killer, at least there was a chance at a million dollar book deal and appearances on national TV. Standing out in front of our room, I briefly considered knocking on the door, leaving the groceries and fleeing. Then I began to wonder if she knew something I didn't.

Could I leave? Changes were obviously taking place in my body that I didn't understand. Maybe I couldn't just go home and pick up where I left off. I missed home but if things worked out, it was still mine and would be forever. I still needed to learn more. I was afraid to look directly into the sun, vertiginously afraid. What else? In the movies, the sun was the big problem. Stake to the heart? Well that would've been bad even before, I know better than to let things piece my body. I didn't like having to trust her. Trust was the hardest thing with others, immortal or not. Did she trust me now despite indicating she'd need my blood later. If I was so intrinsic how could she let me out of her sight?

Without further consideration, I opened the door and stepped back inside. She wasn't on the bed or in the bathroom. I searched frantically for a note or indication of what happened. I went back out. The stolen truck was still there. I scanned the lot to no avail. About to turn back to the room, kick the door shut and scream out into the rural early morning emptiness, I heard her voice. She was telling me to shut the door, I was letting the sun in.

She beckoned from beneath the bed in the parched whisper which made all the hairs on the back of my neck stand up and reach out for communion with this woman, this creature. Wrapped head to toe in the blanket, she awaited my return and I loved her for being there.

"I'm sorry." I closed the offending door, keeping out the harsh horrible light of morning then used whatever was around to block out as much of the sun as possible.

About to step up on the bed and take down a bland faux oil panting from the wall to put in front of the window, she reached out for my ankle.

"I need you, Blood Lover," she whispered. I slid under the bed and felt oddly comfortable in the dark tight space. Her limbs curled around me as I sought her in the blanket. She was cold as stone, cold inside and out, an intense and alien, deathlike chill enveloped me carrying the experience beyond mere sensuousness.

In this cool ecstasy, I was able to bear her biting into the flesh in the hollow of my cheekbones, my earlobe the soft shoulder and pectoral muscles.

There was a saltiness in her kisses, I'm certain was blood and I sought it out over and over to follow whatever path fate had lain before me.

Later that evening, I woke and rolled out from under the bed. I was weak and frail. I looked like hell, bony and wounded everywhere. My fingernails had turned a dull blue gray.

Night had fallen and seemed heavy, permanent and tangible. I felt lighter, spry. I moved through the night air as if I could step up into the darkness and swim through it, drift in its current forever and away from, morning, from daylight and my life.

While spinning on one toe over and over to see how many revolutions I could make, the door burst open. A burly man in stained overalls and a baseball cap came through the door reeking of beer, sweat and piss. Over his shoulder, he carried Drucilla, her slender ankles and calves against his barrel deep chest.

"I'm 'bout ta spread you like bad news." He stopped yammering when she suddenly leapt away and slammed the door shut. In the light coming from the bathroom I saw him fumble with a lamp.

"Pay close attention this time," Drew said, probably talking to me.

When her guest managed to turn on the lamp she was standing directly in front of him. In an instant she struck out, her hand like a spear ending in coarsely sharpened nails.

She yanked blood vessels from his neck and severed them with a flick of her wrist. Blood sprayed out in a thick semi circle and the man twisted away from her an entire second too late.

She kicked his legs out from under him. He fell with a hard thud shaking the entire room, causing the mirror to fall off the tiny vanity and shatter on the back of the chair nearby. In another moment I heard the horrible slurping.

"Come over here, you have to feed today," she told me, dark blood dripping from her mouth in fine streams.

"You want me to start drinking *his* blood?" I asked even as the answer was obvious.

"You have to get used to it if you are to make it on your own," she answered. There was something incredibly bleak about those words.

It seemed the moment blurred, time crawled at a low growling whine. I dropped to my knees and watched the man in slight dismay, watched his half hearted hopeless pulse push blood into the cool air. There was something inside me, not exactly a hunger or a pang but a painful little cramp blossoming within at the smell of fresh blood.

The wrist seemed a neutral spot to start off with and when I touched it, it sprang into action and started to flail blindly, stubby dirty fingers came close to putting out my eye.

Drucilla braced him with a boot in his armpit then opened the wrist with her dangerous nails. I drank in the warmth and was bathed in it, closed my eyes and tumbled through blackness euphoric with nostalgia, reeling with every adolescent grasp of eternity.

In the next instant it was a terrible splashdown into an ocean of blood inhabited by other hideous beings of shear bone and muscle wading and bobbing in the deep crimson pitch under a nebula streaked dome of darkness.

When it seemed every buoyant beast had turned a collective grimace towards me in recognition, I pulled away.

The man who had burst through the door in what seemed to be a segment of a recollected dream, laid still and dead before me, the ruddy redness lost from his cheeks, eyes wide open and opaque.

He had come expecting the transient bliss of sex and found final swift and brutal terror instead. I turned to Drucilla who had become more radiant and alluring than I'd ever seen.

I could only imagine that I, having drank from the same vessel, must have looked just as vital, for she kissed me on the lips. An uplifting current flowed between us, my eyelids seemed to peal away as I stared relentlessly into and through her to the horizon above the crimson pitch on the planet of blood I'd glimpsed earlier. In my bloodstream an omnipotent exuberance pulsed through my body.

"Welcome to the Sang Gang," she whispered as she broke the embrace. "Never to feel daylight, never to bear young, never to fear time nor tide nor beast nor man nor god," she said in tones evocative of fanfare and pageantry.

"What were you saying before about being on my own?" I asked.

"We're not bound to each other and I have made good on my promise," she said stepping away to start gathering all she wanted to take with her.

"I don't feel that I am ready. There are things I really need to know. Things you have to show me."

"So, you will stay by my side, help me?" she paused to watch for my answer.

"Certainly. We will help each other."

"I walked away from that wreck for one reason. I seek revenge," she stated, an inhuman flatness to her voice.

"Oh," I said.

"If you are to stay by my side, you are to help me find a woman in her grave. You must help me destroy her for leaving me to rot."

"We're going to kill a dead chick?" I asked, peering out into the new ceaseless night that was to be my world.

# 5

# THE MAN WHO KILLED MY SISTER

## 2008

Strands of unwashed black hair blew across the top of his head like a filthy plume of factory smoke in the wind tearing across the railroad's elevated platform at Forest Hills. I had never been to this part of Queens, it looked like an old world European village; the way I pictured Vienna.

I've been following this man for a week, making mental notes about his activity and cataloging the types of people he had contact with. I even jotted some of it down but didn't know why or what to do with the information. The details of the man's life were meaningless to me save one; he was the man who killed my sister.

The police did nothing because there wasn't enough proof. One wiseass detective had pulled me aside during my hysterical siege on the precinct and leveled with me. He'd given me a cup of sweet cool coffee and sat me down at a desk in the corner of the room away from the hub-bub and activity.

He sat, elbows on the desk, folded his hands together and rested his chin on the braid of knuckles. Blank, he gazed at me a few moments in consideration as I squirmed anxiously.

"I know this isn't an easy time for you or your family. It's Paul, right? I remember you from February."

"I know. That's why I kept coming to you," I explained flatly.

"Well, I wanted to talk to you before, kind of off the record, so to speak," he said trying gauge my reaction to his words carefully.

"Do you know something about Anna?" I asked.

"I know things I haven't said, things about her case and this department, about police work in general. Things which may or may not be helpful."

"Why have you waited? You kept telling me you were doing all you could, so what the fuck?" I demanded shrilly.

"Like I said. Off the record, unofficial. Things that go outside the realm of police work. things I wouldn't normally say," he explained.

Although glaring, I sipped the coffee to let him know I was still patiently going to give him a chance despite my outburst. "Missing person cases don't get much attention without some evidence of foul play," he began.

"You said that before. My kid sister starts hanging out with an old sleazy creep, she disappears from her house taking nothing with her and leaves no word, note or clue. You don't think there's been foul play?"

"I think there's been foul play. You're hurt, your family is hurt but I have no proof anything happened to her. Not enough proof for the kind of investigation you want to take place," he said.

"I read once that women are mostly killed by the men they know. It's all over the papers. When a young woman is murdered the man in her life is the prime suspect."

"Yes, murdered, maimed, beaten. We'd be all over it if there was a body, a body part, blood, a threatening voicemail...something."

"I saw them together, I saw the way he looked at her," I said slowly.

"Listen, I have a younger sister. I remember feeling that way when I was your age. You get used to that. Sisters are women too." "I won't get used to it, Anna is gone."

At this his chin sank back down on his bony knuckles. He sat there and looked around the room a few moments, the window, a bony underdressed woman straining against her handcuffs as another officer tried to collect her personal information.

"Remember me telling you that we had nothing to go on regarding D. Strobos; the man you thought we should question. I told you we didn't even have enough information to be sure he even existed. You were the only one who saw him, you couldn't recall his first name. Just that it started with a D. There was nothing on her cell phone record, no emails, nothing in her personal effects.

None of her friends ever heard of him. For a few moments, some of my co-workers even thought you might have known something you didn't say, but I didn't think so. I believed you could be right. The only thing is, this department isn't going to budge just because we *think* you could be right."

"If there is nothing to go on, why do you believe me?" I asked, trying to understand what he thought I should know.

"I didn't say there was *nothing*. There isn't enough. There's a criteria. There are shifts, there is a budget."

"What are you not telling me?" I got up and glowered ineffectively.

"*Donny Strobos*. There was a report filled a few years ago, in Manhattan. There was a grisly murder.

Another young woman," he stated distantly as he was still tossing ideas back and forth in his head.

"So why isn't there a full scale investigation?"

"The murder was solved, the guilty party has been institutionalized," the detective said.

"It's not so, I've seen Strobos with my sister!"

"Calm down. The man locked away is an ex police officer, not D. Strobos. He'd stalked her. They found him outside the victim's apartment disoriented, confused. His story didn't work, there were loose ends but the jury had heard enough from the DA."

"What was in the report?" I asked, having become a bit confused myself.

"Prior to her death, the victim had filled a report saying this man, Donny Strobos had jumped out her eighth floor window. It said they'd met through a personal ad."

"I don't understand."

"Neither do we."

"Are you saying this guy died a few years ago?"

"No. All I'm saying is this. Life has a lot of details. Not all of them have meaning. More often than not, the clues and leads we find are meaningless to the case. The name D. Strobos could be a meaningless coincidence," he explained.

"Do you believe that?"

"I don't know."

"So what is this about?"

"I can see you're not ready to let this go. I don't want to see you in any trouble. Now, I know what I'd do in your place but being sure is very important. If you turn anything up, I want to know. I want you to be discreet. Call the number on my card. Don't do anything. The other thing I have that is as close to the big nothing that you have… I know the ex cop in the nut house. We were at the academy together. It was a while ago, but he was a good guy, not a nut. Something happened. It had to. There were way too many loose ends."

I had left the precinct, feeling good for the first time in weeks. I knew I wasn't crazy. I had gone back to Anna's room, did my best to ignore my grieving mother, and looked for anything that could help me find Donny Strobos.

There were all sorts of new things in her life since she'd come back from school. Anna had studied abroad, been to India and Sri Lanka. Scattered about her room were little Eastern gee-gaws, foreign books, packs of clove cigarettes and a dirty hookah. She had been spouting liberal propaganda about the Middle East that would have pissed our father off something fierce if he was still around. Mom figured it was just a phase she'd pass through and leave behind eventually.

Anna had multiple piercings, she had started to wear black and go to subtitled movies.

She had become a weirdo. I complained that her school was too liberal and it seemed there were too few honest educational requirements; but she was the first in our family to go to college so nothing could defray the excitement and enthusiasm, especially since her grades were high.

I found the few old issues of the *Village Voice* she had saved. The personal ad section must have gone digital. I was disappointed at first, until I realized they were more accessible and informative online. I knew I was on to something. I scoured the columns for hours, reading, re-reading, looking to see if anything rang a bell as familiar or curious. I wondered if the police had looked into this, recalling what I had been told about the other victim.

In Anna's computer, I finally found something useful. She had made note of a password used for Craigslist and Backpages accounts. I couldn't find anything by searching her number on the Backpages but found her Craigslist posting. I clicked in fear of what I'd read but it was an innocent ad. I felt horribly intrusive but had to continue. I read the posting and wept thinking about her hopeful words reaching out for freaky friendship. She sought other young people interested in what she called *happenings* and avant garde cinema. I had checked her voicemail over and over it was still empty.

Perhaps she deleted the messages after hearing them. I didn't know.

What did the geniuses at the precinct make of the young women running away without their smartphones? Maybe it was a dead end. They already checked the phone out, maybe not as many times as I have but there didn't seem to be anything relevant anyway.

I didn't know what made me feel worse; that my sister was putting ads on web filth like the Backpages and Craigslist or that it seemed no-one had answered them.

Nearly four years ago, when our father passed away, I took a job in a wheelchair factory outside Trenton where he'd worked. Everyone knew him and his reputation had smoothed a path there for me. When I told them I needed some time off because of Anna, they understood.

The floor manager had guaranteed my position would be open for me when I came back. He had sat me down and we traded anecdotes about my old man over scotch.

Before I left, he folded five hundred dollars into my hand and held it there a moment. "This should help you get on," he said, before letting go.

I spent weeks studying everything, unwilling to let any possibility, however so slim, get by me. I followed each clue to its terminus, left no stone unturned.

In the day, I loitered in and around every store or little shop Anna had shopping bags or receipts from. I talked to each of her friends and snooped on their friends and family. In the evenings, I perched on barstools, sipped beers in all the lounges and bars she had cute matchbooks from, looking for her killer.

I spent a lot of the bar time trying to sketch a workable likeness of the fiend. It was difficult. I could picture his face; I knew him when I saw him. In a drawing I couldn't capture the way his jaw moved under his skin, or the way his eyes seemed to pick up and fix on you if you looked in his direction from almost anywhere in his periphery. It was one of those initial things which bothered me about him.

I recalled getting off the bus the first evening I had seen him with Anna. They were waiting for the bus going into New York, across the street from my stop. We hadn't met and Anna hadn't seen me, but Strobos noticed my attention, returned and held my gaze. There was a momentary flash of something terrible, a perilously bad feeling. He had the wild feral eyes of a wounded animal and they were often quite bloodshot.

More than a month had passed before I found him. Having almost run out of funds, I had began to wander about the areas where Anna spent her last weeks. In a little pocket on the inside of her new lavender raincoat, there were ticket stubs from the Cinemart Theatre. It was in Forest Hills. It was not too far from where I stood tonight, avoiding the puddles of brightness cast by the line of ancient-looking gaslights on the railroad's platform.

The Cinemart played the kind of arty films that Anna had been calling avant garde cinema. She had been saving the stubs from her favorites but I had never seen these amongst them. They must have been recent; one from something called *Nightwatch* and another from *Cashe.* Both were dated for Thursdays in early February, before I'd seen her with Strobos. I checked them out nevertheless.

Right next door to the theater was a trendy-looking cafe that had my sister written all over it. There were cozy tables, plush leather, salads and fancy coffees. There were slim middle-aged fags and Eurotrash wannabees gesticulating on espresso.

When I showed the waitress my sister's picture, she recognized her. She knew her name. When I told her that Anna was missing she sat down quietly for a moment. I had to practically beg her to talk, citing our fears, my mother's harried grief.

She told me Anna had been hanging out with a Dion Strobos, the part time projectionist from the neighboring Cinemart Theatre.

Reluctantly, she informed me that she knew he had called in sick the week of Anna's initial disappearance. She thought the couple had just broken up and that Dion, whom she'd described as a quiet, sensitive type, just needed some time to recover.

I found it difficult not to storm the theater. I called my new friend at the precinct like he'd told me to. I got his voicemail but decided not to leave a message. I wasn't sure what I wanted to say, what I wanted the police to have a record of at that point. Detective Amano not only seemed like a good guy but I was under the impression that he wanted something done. Not only for the women who fell prey to this beast but for an old friend and fellow lawman. He knew I couldn't leave it alone. He knew I couldn't wait for the wheels of justice to be spun by the long arm of the law.

Dion Strobos or Donny Strobos worked from eight to one AM, four nights a week.

I had been carrying a tremendous survival blade strapped to my ankle, the kind that Sylvester Stallone had in the *Rambo* movies. It had a nasty-looking serrated edge and a hollow handle stocked with waterproof matches and a first aid kit. I purchased a ticket for the 9:40PM  showing of *A Battle in Heaven* and planned to confront and or kill him while he was alone in the dark and might not be discovered for a couple of hours.

I had considered going to see Amano in the morning if it worked out. I would give him a signal of sorts letting him know that a big loose end had been clipped. How could he betray me? How could he deny me my revenge? I had been imagining that he knew my intentions, that he approved and would cover my tracks but couldn't just come out and say the words.

As soon as the previews ended, I got up from my seat with the unsheathed blade in my coat pocket. Carefully, I approached one of the projectionist booths but the door was locked. They all were. I had to wait it out.

I thought I sat down in the wrong auditorium because the movie didn't seem like anything about heaven. It was fat Mexicans having sex then a man who urinates on himself kills a friendly hooker with a kitchen knife. I had dozed off towards the end. I searched the place but it seemed Strobos was gone.

Staking out the Cinemart proved to be more effective. I started to follow him. I had kept my distance and then some, plodding along with a vagrant's lack of purpose while trying not to be conspicuous on the sparsely traveled residential streets and shuttered shops.

It was dark and quiet enough. I could knife him if I dared get close but I didn't. It wasn't fear of his uncanny sense of awareness but rather curiosity. How could this man kill my sister, calmly do his job and walk the streets as if it had no meaning?

What if it wasn't him and they had broken up, as the waitress at the cafe thought? I wanted to know if he had friends or cohorts. I wanted to know as much as I could find out to be certain he was the one.

I watched him travel his route after the theater shift. There were little variances, but there was a routine. I kept a small notebook and made a number of entries that helped me stay on his trail without having to follow his direct path.

Just before dawn, he would cross a ten-lane expressway the local press dubbed the "Boulevard of Death" because of the number of pedestrian fatalities. Then he'd walk down Jewell Avenue. Behind the garage of a house with a for sale sign sprouting from its lawn, Strobos would snake in through a small window and crash for the balance of the night. I considered following him in one morning but it seem risky to walk into the fiend's lair. I toyed with the idea of setting the house on fire but there was no guarantee I'd get him.

Tonight wasn't too different from the others. First, he walked to Austin Street which was lined by a number of restaurants and bars with constant patronage in the evenings.

His first stop was a small wine bar. He lingered at the window until a woman came out. She was older, perhaps late forties but slim, still attractive and dressed to accent her svelte figure.

Wordlessly, she followed Strobos to a nearby doorway. They disappeared in shadow. By the time I got close enough to investigate the woman was back on the street. She lit a cigarette but didn't smoke it. Her breathing was a little labored. I could see her exhale in the cool March night.

Almost miraculously, I'd seen Strobos further up the street, his pace livelier. I couldn't have missed him. To get ahead of her, almost a block away, he would have had to enter a building, use an alleyway door, sprint down the alley, then come out on the other end of the block.

I didn't understand what had gone on. Were they lovers or friends? Did he have something for her, a message perhaps? It seemed seedy, not out of the realm of expectations I had for the fiend. Whatever was going on, I'm sure it was wrong.

Further down Austin Street, he made another stop. He stood outside a shop, the kind that sold expensive khakis, forty flavors of blue jeans and colorful fag shirts. It was closed but there was movement inside, stock or inventory work. There was the flash of something gold, a pocket watch. He looked at it for a moment then snapped it shut at the sound of a deadbolt and a jangling cluster of keys. A twenty-something goth chick teetering on four inch clunky boots came out and hugged him tightly. I passed them on the opposite side of the street. There was a moment when I suspected he saw me but couldn't be certain, his face was obscured by her thick bolts of her shoulder-length black and green hair.

I'd stood at the corner obeying the crosswalk signal despite the nearly nonexistent traffic. The couple walked to a car parked in darkness beneath the nearby railroad trestle. She opened the driver's side door and got in. She started the car and immediately turned on music loud enough for me to hear as I crossed the street, a syncopated headbanger with shrieking women on the vocals. The sound was muffled and the map light went out as Strobos closed his door. There was a small news stand still open which afforded me a bit of cover. I entered and pretended to consider the magazines and mints.

Again the interaction had been brief.

According to the waitress he had been spending more time with Anna. Perhaps he was trying to replace her but why the late night interludes?

There were sometimes as many as three other stops he'd make in the area, ending usually after 4 AM or so. What did this weird Don Juan do with all these women for five or six minutes? Each meeting seemed to energize him. He seemed more vital or unrealistically lively after each interaction. I imagined only sex or money could do that to a man.

There was only one plausible explanation to me. Strobos was a drug dealer. He was a horrible sort who went around corrupting the young and enabling the troubled. The conclusion renewed my vengeful spirit. I knew what I wanted and knew what his last stop was every Thursday night. It was almost time. I could see him consult his pocket watch again.

The eastbound train was late. He was waiting for a nurse or doctor; a mature Asian woman who wore light green scrubs and white rubber clogs under her coat. I felt the cruel edge of the blade with my thumb.

There was no sign of the train.

I pulled my watch cap down nearly to the bridge of my nose and propped up the collar of my jacket. Even if he did recognize me, the only reason he should attempt flight would be his guilt.

You didn't just do away with a guy's sister and then expect to make small talk on a deserted train station platform at a quarter after four in the morning.

I stepped from a shadow and casually approached him, ready with the obvious question about where the train was. He didn't move at first then turned towards me. I could feel his eyes lock on. He took his hands out of his pockets and let them dangle loosely at his sides. As I approached, he didn't react in either fear or recognition. A tired half smile briefly crossed his face. "Paulie," he said, as Anna used to call me.

He didn't react when the ugly blade became visible in my hand.

"Have you found what you wanted these nights?" he asked me, making me certain he'd been aware of my presence all along.

"I'm gonna fucking gut you, for what you did to Anna!" I rushed him and he sidestepped me elegantly, three or four times. An onlooker would have thought we were dancing, or performing a choreographed fight scene like the one James Dean did in *Rebel Without a Cause.*

Close to him, he seemed bigger. His blood vessels must have burst. The whites of both eyes were crimson and creepy.

"I miss her as well," he said and disarmed me deftly. Weaponless, I had only two choices. I jumped on him but he didn't go down. Awestruck for a moment by his strength, he tossed me hard onto the platform, a petty annoyance.

"I'm gonna kill you!" I half sob-screamed.

"She would have come for you, your mother, her friends. You wouldn't have been able to stop her. She'd be eating your heart with her bare hands before you even thought about fighting back," he said then looked over his shoulder for a sign of the train's arrival.

I got up again and made a move. Strobos slipped from my grasp and stayed behind me. No matter how hard I tried I could not turn to face him, he was too fast.

"What are you on, you sick fuck?"

"I'm high on life," I heard him say.

"What did you give her?" I demanded, "Why her? Didn't you like her?" I said, feeling an inescapable hopelessness welling up inside. I could hear him sniffing the air loudly, purposefully.

"I can smell your fear, the collapse of your soul. This is not your day to break free." His words cryptic as he tossed the blade at my feet.

"If vengeance doth sate thine blood, so be it." He continued, probably trying to confuse or distract me with theatrics. In the cold wind, he stripped off his tattered pinstripe blazer and dark hooded sweatshirt. If the creep's insanity, guilt or drug abuse would let me find justice for Anna and who knows how many others, then so be it, I thought, his words echoing in my mind. He had stripped off his dingy T-shirt as I picked up the blade. There was light coming down the track on the other platform. His skin, the color of full moon, was crisscrossed with a disturbing amount of scar tissue, some thick, jagged, bold and disgusting.

As the westbound express howled past the station, I jammed the blade, double fisted overhand, into his chest and rode the hilt with all my weight. It seemed that we fell together for an eternal moment, the air crystalizing around me; distinct molecules wheeling around past each other, interlocking like subatomic gears of reality, spinning past each other until I hit the platform. My teeth grinding painfully, I was still bearing down on the blade with both fists, twisting and churning, hoping to rip his cold fucking heart to shreds in the thick dark blood spreading between us.

I looked to his eyes to see if life was finally gone from them. The whites of his eyes were clear, I thought fleetingly, before being held fast by what I saw reflected in the black glassiness of his pupils. Instead of the fearful grimace I could feel in the muscles of my face, there was an impossible vista. It was a bird's eye view of an endless globular city of perilous bridges and confusing systems of intersecting walkways circling a black void. It resembled an M.C. Escher drawing numbly navigated by droves of broken ghouls.

There was more light. The train from Penn Station was finally arriving. I broke free and ran for the stairs, not wanting to be found with the bloody corpse of a drug dealer on the platform. The blade's handle was so coated in blood that I didn't believe a fingerprint could be lifted from it.

I emptied my coat pockets into my pants and ditched my bloody jacket in a trash can in the subway station. Shakily, I rode the E train into Manhattan then waited for a Jersey bound bus at the Port Authority.

There had been nothing in the papers or on TV. I searched each afternoon while getting shit-hammered on boilermakers.

Weeks later, I was back at the factory, the dismal grind of life feeling almost uninterrupted. Often, I find myself thanking the almighty for stand up guys like Detective Amano who surely covered up any link between me and the killing. I'm sure he steered the NYPD in another direction. I never contacted him after that with any information. I'm sure he preferred it that way, just the two of us knowing in silent satisfaction that some form of justice has been done. Months fell from the calendar. I welded endless lines of wheelchair frames together. Sometimes as the cluster os sparks bounces off the my mask I recall what surely was a glimpse of Hell I'd caught in the dead fiend's eyes.

*General.*

*This record named 6th Void, is compiled from video communication logs sent to a woman's family and friends. Initially thought to be delusional, she spoke about an odd locus in space to where she and other entangled persons might have disappeared, although she claims to have spent the time simultaneously in a tomb here in the United States.*

*Filled with idealized romanticism, I planned on dismissing it until I found a newspaper article about a young woman named Alice Perry who walked out of a crypt during a service, scaring onlookers at funeral. I checked the facts from the news. They confirm the identity of a young woman who went missing in the late 1990's. We have emails she sent to her relatives claiming she had been infected with what she called biological vampirism but preferred being entombed to living on blood. She is being sought for questioning. Her testimonials indicate that she may be an accomplice and not one of the entangled as she claims to be infected with a form of vampirism from suspect Strobos.*

*It also confirms what has been said of his motivations with female victims. Mere mayhem may not be his only agenda despite the evidence of extreme violence. And what is it said of music and the savage beast? The Perry woman wrote that he played woodwinds like a snake charmer confirming a detail about our killer mentioned in the Taxi dispatcher's account. If even a discarded reed from his saxophone could be found, we'd have DNA evidence.*

*There are many items for continued research, blood toxicology reports, crystallized hemoglobin samples, some very advanced personal electronic gear, photos of a huge spherical drone that had been seen haunting the graveyard surrounding Ms. Perry's crypt, which matches the description of the drone spoke of by others.*

*I am beginning to think we are close to something, General. I have been studying the evidence around the clock and admittedly observe the circumstantial nature of the connections I'm building in this case, but feel I am on the verge of significant insight.*

*SSgt. F. Chandrastakar*
*Division of Forensic Studies*

6

# The Sixth Void Of Lost Hopes

## 2019

There is no god and there is no Hell, allegorically speaking but there is however, eternity. If eternity has custodians they are concepts and constants, empirical dogma and algorithmic formulae.

Just as Newtonian Law governs the descent of apples from the earth bound boughs of countless orchards and gardens, the universe and its kaleidoscopic intersections of diminishing perspectives, spiraling out though eternity, as home to every possibility, is based on some incontrovertible mathematic principle.

The price one paid for eternity was knowledge of other possibilities; other stations along an infinite axis unfolding forever at ninety degree angles into the myriad of otherwise unseen and unexperienced dimensions of happenstance. This is the way Strobos explained it but it still feels like Hell to me.

We wander in a practically ceaseless stupor upon an impossible network of walkways, bridges and inverted jetties orbiting the black dodecahedron of netherspace known as the Sixth Void. Here, we spend centuries viewing the long term realities that never can occur in the life spans of the mortals that had been close to us or the awful things they endure due to our absence from the brief pageantry of humanity.

If we don't suffer seeing the misfortune our loved ones endure in our wakes, we're forced to bear the many ways their lives were improved as a result of our disappearances.

I had just watched the lonely death of an old high school friend who had a skiing accident on a Colorado slope. Alone, she was never found and froze to death in agony. My plans to join her on the trip changed after meeting Strobos and contracting what I had long referred to as the special morning sickness. Sunrise would bring on a nausea and a vertiginous sense of destruction's certainty, which made daytime and daylight activity forever forbidden to me.

Soon, I expect to witness the saga of that same friend's happy marriage to a man from our neighborhood whom I had been certain to wed but didn't. There was no way to know which of these life paths she really lived. It was torment meticulously culled somehow from memories.

We are not the dead amongst the undead, which was another one of his arguments against the Sixth Void being Hell. There are no destroyed vampires among our numbers. For a vampire to be destroyed was to cease being from that moment forward on any plane of existence.

We are all caught in helpless stasis either as a result of a botched slaying or other unfortunate turn of events. Some are entombed and weakened, staked and bloodless. Others lie dormant, trapped, not properly beheaded or incinerated.

My body lies undamaged among the earth's Great Entombed. Despite how difficult it can be for one of us to find a mate, many of the Great Entombed are as such due to a failed relationship.

I had been made an immortal by Dionysis Strobos in the mid 1980's. We had met as a result of an ad he had placed in a weekly publication called the *Boston Phoenix*.

A friend had responded to it for me as a joke. When Strobos and I talked on the phone, he didn't sound insane or pathetic like they expected. He had been romantic, educated and multilingual. As a twenty four year old grad student from Wisconsin, he was the most different kind of man I had ever encountered. He possessed the casual gallantry of a film star, intellect that rivaled my professors on some topics and was always generous with everyone.

Even now, in this horrid place, I still fondly recall our first encounter. I had that warm fuzzy feeling which allowed him such immediate intimacy, recalled how gentle his hands were, running his fingers through my hair as he complemented me as no midwesterner ever did.

We had spent nights strolling in the moonlight on the banks of the Charles River, talking practically until daybreak when he would walk me home to the apartment I shared with another student in Boston's Back Bay.

Our courtship had been completely nocturnal. Dion had explained that he had just started a position working an early shift at a blood bank and couldn't get days off for a while.

The only things I had found odd was that he had no friends of his own in the area and he usually wore the same few pieces of clothing in different combinations, every time I saw him. He wore shades often at night and not just after six or seven PM but well after midnight. A number of my friends thought he was creepy and a bit pretentious but they really didn't know him, his contentedness with simple pleasures and his patience.

My roommate's cat was another thing altogether. Before Strobos would even enter a room, Tangy would practically climb up the walls. I know now the panicked cat was really looking to jump dimensions, aware of the open pathways in an immortal's wake.

Looking back, I wish she had. Although it was a couple of decades ago, I can still hear the shrieks and the uneven grinding of the electric juicer, still taste her fresh, warm and frothy blood.

This existence, this never ending sleepwalk and the terrible desires made me want to kill myself, which makes being entombed for eternity seem so appropriate despite Strobos and his disappointment.

Facing the void once again, having closed my eyes, a minute detail is rendered before me as large as a planet, as large as a gas giant like Saturn.

It is the salty devastation collecting in the corner of my father's eye. Reflected in that warm anguished teardrop were the twisting rusty loops of the chain link fence his body sagged against as he secretly watched the graduation procession I would have taken part in if Strobos hadn't met me.

Above ground, in a small granite and stainless steel edifice I know is bathed in beautiful sunlight for hours, my body lies awaiting our special dinners and the blood kiss that keeps me from having to battle the pangs to do the ungodly.

Unlike so many others that have caught his attention, I arose from the dead psychologically unchanged. We had celebrated traveling through Europe by train, spent days behind the thick curtains and shutters of our sleeping cars, reading magazines and watching DVD's. By night we'd stroll through ancient cities buying souvenirs and flowers to bring back to our compartment on the train.

In his ancient homeland, there was an old man named Fotis who kept a small cottage for him and watched over us during the day. He'd picked us up in Turkey by motorboat and carried us through the darkness to Greece. There we moon bathed, shared dreams and spooned on the pale seaside cliffs of Mykonos.

Strobos would go out and feed on goats or wayward tourists. Upon returning, he would bite his tongue, practically perforate it with his canines. I would feed like his baby bird.

He'd hold me bundled in his arms for an hour or so, just as he had earlier to make me a vampire, I'd feed on the dizzying saltiness in his kiss.

The problems started when I wouldn't feed on humans myself. A vampire couldn't live by merely feeding on another vampire. Not exactly as futile as an *Ouroboros*, the serpent eating its tail, we could sustain ourselves for only so long without the blood of the living. Human blood wasn't a requirement, but there was only so much animal blood our system's could use before it became an issue. Animal blood is missing the components necessary to maintain a human body. If you spot an immortal whose body is rotting or will not heal, its diet is only animal blood.

Turning away from the void in this eternal nightmare, I paced a walkway and greeted those I knew and ignored others for the same reasons. There were those who gather and suffer together, usually the ones who were languishing lost somewhere without hope of human contact or the improper slaying attempts left nearly bloodless, weak and confined.

There is another woman in a predicament similar to mine who has become my strolling companion over the years. Her body has been sealed in a black glass coffin by her family in the 1890's when her husband discovered her feeding on his horses at night. The dark glass and gold framed case lies in at the bottom of a pond on property still owned by the same family today. Her secret died with her husband and brother in Poland at the hands of the Nazi's in the 1930's.

Tall blonde and beautiful, I find my friend Veronika, gazing out at nebula streaked space on the same jetty every two weeks or so. She spends as little time as possible staring back into the Sixth Void. Most of what she sees is the senseless brutality the Germans perpetrated upon her country and the deaths of those close to her she could have prevented had she not been sealed in glass and dropped to remain in murky waters so close to her family's home.

Today a new distress crossed her face but it was news for me which worried her so. Occasionally, one of us returns to the world they came from, just as new vampires arrive after dire calamity. Despite my very brief interaction with the world of immortals, I have an enemy.

It was a woman Strobos had changed long before me, a woman whom as a vampire feeds in a shark like manner, always on the move, desperate and crazed like a fugitive. Known only as Drucilla, She took pleasure in almost nothing but the hunt, a woman who once vied for the leadership of the New England Sang Gang, a band of roving creatures posing as bikers who had once welcomed her and Strobos to ride and camp with them in rural Massachusetts and New Hampshire.

Strobos didn't like to hunt in a pack, preferred hotels to the woods and couldn't get used to the fireside orgies, rape, torture and murders that would pass for entertainment at midnight.

For Drucilla, the Sang Gang felt like home, so Strobos left her to enjoy the mayhem.

When she met me in the Sixth Void and we shared our stories, she was jealous in hearing about how Strobos would visit my crypt, nourish me and bring gifts to help pass the time. She didn't believe I'd told Strobos about her problem because he hadn't rescued her.

Veronika not only told me Drucilla been set free to roam the earth once more but that she vows vengeance on us both.

*General,*

*We live in a time where human longevity has become increasingly important with the advent of real space travel. Odd, old folklore, legends and fiction based on folklore describing methods for extending life or sentient existence has become very popular. It is not hard to imagine a sect of humans perceiving vampirism as a disease or even a beneficial mutation for an organism.*

*I remember a filmstrip shown in an anthropology course from my university years. New Guinea, I believe or perhaps Madagascar. An Indigenous klatch of young hunters had just slain a boar. They drank the fresh blood, frothy from the frantic fight or flight failure as I looked on appalled, until hearing the professors's explanation. The blood of the living carries nutrition, making it the most vital and healthy yield of the kill. With this in mind, it isn't difficult for me to imagine any number of the entangled abandoning vitamin supplements for take- out from their local blood bank.*

*Further forensic insight into systems of religious beliefs in Western culture supports a familiarity or even acceptance of vampiric immortality as some Christian services involve the promise of everlasting life as a benefit from drinking the blood of their savior. I have theorized a model wherein Suspect Strobos uses these ingrained concepts and rituals to mask or distract his intended victims and or accomplices from discerning his true malign intent.*

*Amongst the entangled, there are a group of persons whose accounts venture far from the normal encounters. I sometimes feel as if we are hunting UFO's. There are numerous reports from people who saw something odd in the middle of the night when they were alone. There are many from people behind bars who claim our suspect to be the true perpetrator of their crimes.*

*Some reports are like the wild tales of those who claim to have been abducted or flown in alien crafts. I will include two that have caught my attention after a brief interview I have scheduled with one man whose tale of entanglement includes information on other entangled parties, which in my opinion could not be known without real collusion with the suspect or his accomplices.*

*SSgt. F. Chandrastakar*
*Division of Forensic Studies*

## 7

# STROBOS ON THE MOON

## 2048

From the narrow strip of tinted Flexiglass lining the interrogation room, the greenHouse deck was visible. I liked to sit down there and watch the Earthrise like a giant blue eye in my dreams. You could lie there for hours and bask in the wild organic reek of various strains of fertilized wheatgrass growing in curving rows all the way to the apparent horizon at the greenHouse's end.

I used to bring a book, a couple of strong liquor gel tubes or hot soup. It was where I'd first encountered Strobos, the reason I'm in custody, waiting for the investigators to tell me what could be confirmed of my story.

Ironically, it was where I was apprehended, weeks later.

Something had to check out. Even if a man could get away from the NewLunar Complex, it didn't mean all his information disappeared as well. If he had been here for the last two months or lunar cycles, he had to leave a trail. Everyone had to eat, had to spend credit on recreation or personal purchases.

As I've had the time to think, I was quite happy Strobos was missing. His sudden absence should be looked upon as flight unless they wanted to accuse me of killing him as well.

As it had become habit, I was awake for every full earthrise. The side of the moon which was home to the NewLunar Complex always faced earth. Because of positioning between the moon and sun it wasn't always visible, much in the way the moon wasn't always visible from earth.

Every two weeks, there were dark days in which either the earth was directly in between the moon and the sun or when the moon came directly between the sun and the earth. It was the opposite of earth's lunar month corresponding to new and full moon phases. As we experience this biweekly cycle, an archaic word describing two weeks was in vogue; *a fortnight*.

Full earth or what we Newlunatics called *terragrande* occured during new moon when the moon was invisible to the earthbound because no sunlight fell upon our side.

Most people busied themselves during this brief sunless period either exercising at the RecCenter to fight muscle atrophy, or hid away in the bars or MediaCenter. I preferred the deck at the greenHouse's end, past the rows of fruit trees and the beeGarden. I'd relax in the peaceful blue light coming from the earth with some cocktail gel tubes and listen to a book with my earphones.

Sometimes, I would just get drunk and watch the wisps of white cloud swirl and spread on the earth's big blue green face. It had been on one of those mornings, when I noticed another. Someone was strolling through the neatly cultivated rows of wheatgrass.

As the figure grew near, I heard music, not the soothing random synthesizer tones that washed over the complex periodically, but live music. It sounded like a clarinet or saxophone, a somber melody. I turned off my audiobook and listened. The climate control came on and cycled the air, filling the greenHouse with the soft brush of leaves on the breeze and carried scents from the surrounding orchards to mingle.

The stranger seemed to appear suddenly and startled me even though I had been anticipating his arrival. It had just seemed too soon. He smiled and played more as if to say *that was me you were listening to.*

The guy was also in his early thirties but of the hipper contingent amongst us who preferred to wear vintage earth apparel and leather boots. Over the dark hooded unitard we all had, he wore a nearly threadbare grey pinstripe three piece suit, pants tucked into crackling leather paratrooper boots.

Although it had been a sunless day, huge dark glasses were part of the outfit. He finished his phrase with a shrill trill and let the instrument hang from its strap around his neck.

"Strobos. Second Phebotomy Unit," he'd said.

"Greysmith, First Construction; Interiors." I stood to shake his hand, expecting some new moon hipster move but he didn't extend a hand.

"I know who you are. I've seen you at Crater with the Sabian sisters. We're a small community, Thump fans, I mean. The other clubs just play old music."

"I know. How many more times can you listen to *Planet Claire* or *Major Tom* before the novelty wears off," I kidded.

We seemed to connect. I offered him a Vodka-tini gel tube but he declined, said he was on a natural high. He told me where to catch the latest tune streams from Shanghai; the thump center of the music world where DJ's first played thump in clubs. Thump was a new loop music which used nature sounds. Different animal heartbeats provided the rhythms. The newest combined hummingbird and blue whale heartbeats with copulating monkey moans, the death shrieks of young swans and hippo burps.

I could tell he was impressed with the Sabian sisters, or maybe he wanted to immediately let me know his orientation to get that out of the way.

When I first heard one of the sisters; Juliana, was missing, I didn't make the connection.

Lots of men were interested in the Sabian Sisters and many had been spurned and angered. When I introduced him, he'd been a big hit with both women but seemed more interested in the older twin; Anastasia.

Anastasia was only twelve minutes older than her fraternal twin yet often acted like Juliana's mother. They were both in their late thirties but spent months, year after year, at NewLunar like many fading beauties who found out how much kinder the moon's lower gravity was to their faces and figures. Visitor patronage to NewLunar's clubs and spas, initially constructed for staff use, practically paid our salaries, which suited our employers just fine.

Anastasia and Strobos had hit it off fabulously which made me very happy at the time. He seemed so well travelled for his age, suiting the heiress and her social set even better than I did.

He and Anastasia would toss pricey liquor gels back and forth into each other's mouths late into the evening while trading witty quips in a dozen or so languages. Genuinely enthused by the scenario, I'd always picked up his tab. With big sister occupied, there was finally opportunity for me explore the possibilities of broadening my relationship with the darker more demure sister, Juliana.

Initially, I had gone to Strobos when I heard Juliana was missing, unaware of his involvement. I'd hoped he could convince her sister I had nothing to do with the disappearance.

A week later, the police turned up some of Juliana's dark hair, a clump complete with its roots. It didn't take long for them to consider me as the culprit. When Anastasia heard about it, one of her family's private security 'bots came after me. When it's all cleared up, I certainly didn't want to pay for the damn thing.

The newer Hyundai-Samsung units were assembled somewhere deep in what was once Mongolia but they cost much more than the previous decade's slower less sentient models. There were a few attached to the investigative unit here at NewLunar and I was lucky enough to have one assigned to my case. If anything or any one could uncover the truth about my innocence, it was one of those units, only I couldn't help but think it had something against me for destroying the one the Sabian family sent after me just a week ago.

The door parted, slid open in narrow sections from the top as another man peered inside. When it was safe to cross the threshold, he did so. It was the other detective, the human of sorts. He seemed to be about my age but was pale and lowG thin from living up here so long. He preferred the moon's gravity to the leg weights just as Strobos did, letting the cop cross the room in a slow and graceful gazelle leap. He sat facing me, lips pursed as if he were waiting for a cue to speak.

"Well?" I prompted. He put his finger over his mouth to silence me.

I stared at him with the leveling contempt of one who could still afford to chose living back on earth. He tilted his head in response to something coming in on his earpiece which made him look all the more ridiculous to me.

He wore his facial hair in the latest NewLunatic fashion; a Hitler mustache with a corresponding stripe of beard running from his lower lip to his chin. The detective had an elongated neck, the rite of passage for those NewLunatics who chose the moon, its darkness and weak gravity as a life option.

He must have been here or at another complex for a more than a decade.

"My supervisor is coming, Greysmith. And it doesn't exactly have good news. More questions," the detective said and smirked. Hearing him describe his boss as *it*, I knew it was one of the new robots I'd heard about.

The 'bot's spectral green face appeared first as the door parted. Ever since 2040 semi- sentient robots were usually composed of plastic, latex and specially engineered organic nervous systems providing a reactive mobility which lets them interact more freely amongst the living in a variety of unpredictable environments. Most were designed in Japan and known as *Semisens*, a very Japanese sounding piece of modern English.

In the security 'bot business, the latest fad was retro looking robots like the kind seen in old science fiction movies more than a century ago. They were large rounded and purposefully mechanical, resembling robots from *Lost in Space* or the *Forbidden Planet*. Atop their broad barrel like chests were cylindrical 3D LCD units used to communicate visual information or broadcast the face of one of its handlers or owners. The term *possessed* was usually used to describe one of these robots that was temporarily being operated by a human who would appear to be looking out at you from the 'bot's head. Other times there would be a spooky greenish hologram.

Private sector security, like the group that operated the Sabian's unit often preferred a simple but frightening talking skull as the 'bot's personality. Law enforcement used dead celebrities. The one on my case spoke through a youngish Basil Rathbone image from his Sherlock Holmes days.

Further enhancing the perception of their individuality, was an irreparable imperfection causing each to develop its own peculiar gait anomaly. Deployment in a variety of environments and gravitational forces eventually caused them all a considerable limp or stagger although no systemic defect could be detected.

Basil Rathbone scanned me as he swayed a bit crossing the room. It seemed to favor its right side, an anomaly consistent with assignment on one of the huge donut shaped orbital stations as a result of centripetal rotation in place of true gravity.

"Greysmith, Adam. Conceived in Hartford Connecticut, United States. 34 years ago?" It confirmed coldly.

"Yes."

"I function as semi sentient Inspector DDF43. You have the right to know that I am monitoring your biofeedback on 3 separate scales as we speak. Understood?" It confirmed.

"Understood."

"Did you knowingly end or interrupt the life and or existence of Juliana Sabian?" It asked me.

"No I did not. I believe it was a man named Strobos from the phlebotomy unit," I answered as clearly and as calmly as I could under the circumstances.

"No record indicates anyone named Strobos was ever employed or attached to this facility in any capacity at any time, nor have the guest rolls listed any such visitor. The phlebotomist on staff at the SleepCenter has been found dead. His body was only identified four hours ago as we searched for the man you described." The 'bot's face went blue and Basil Rathbone was replaced by a youngish red haired man. "This is Norbert Kates, he was the second unit's phlebotomist at the SleepCenter. His body was found on the same transport you took after your last recreation pass," the 'bot said. The other detective took note of this on his wrist PC then stood up and lit a clove cigarette.

"Shaking your tree yet, Cowpoke?" he asked, exhaling the pungent smoke at me. Anytime people spoke to each other around a semisens and didn't want to be understood they used cryptic or archaic slang and expressions.

"Did you encounter this man, Mr. Greysmith?" the 'bot asked.

"Never. Never saw him before in my life," I answered while shooting daggers at the detective who was childishly playing with his eery low gravity smoke rings. The 'bot's head went blue again for a second then played a silent video clip. It was me at the bar on the transport about a month ago. Two stools away sat the dead man, Norbert Kates. I could clearly be seen in a verbal exchange that ended with a bit of sneering profanity on my part.

Dimly, I recalled the incident. We'd been drunken strangers in a brief heated debate over something now forgotten which had only been important during those brief moments of public inebriation.

"The clip clearly depicts you and the deceased in an altercation," the 'bot droned, facelessly.

"I can explain that! I mean, I can't explain the reasons behind it but it was nothing. I didn't even know his name. It was nothing," I insisted.

"The biofeedback detected during this interview is inconclusive as is evidence of your innocence, Mr. Greysmith." The 'bot's big head swiveled around completely to address his human co-worker. "Detective Lowe, Mr. Greysmith is to be remanded to holding for the next 24 hours pending further investigation."

"Right," he said then exhaled clove smoke through his tear ducts like a teenager trying to show off his otherworldly hipness.

This was it. It was to be made official. Detective Lowe cuffed me then lead me through a few narrow corridors, executing fluid leaps and mid air spins like an Olympic figure skater. At the end of the last corridor, a window opened and a uniformed officer demagnetized the handcuffs to allowing me to surrender my personal effects and make a call.

I didn't have a lawyer and I honestly didn't expect anyone who knew me back on earth to make the trip up here to comfort me until I was cleared.

If there was bail to make, I would consider it at the time of my sentencing. If it was murder they charged me with, I don't imagine being able to make the bail anyway. Not one to waste a free phone call, I called the last woman I'd slept with. She had learned to hate me over the span of our courtship, so the news should be entertaining. She could go around for a year or more telling people how right she was for dumping a psycho loser like me, while chortling over cocktails in one of the new floating clubs in Shanghai. She wasn't home so I left a message. Attempt to hear a friendly or at least familiar voice having failed, I marched obediently to my cell to await further information. I was innocent and had time off from work. How bad could it get?

The space was nearly a two meter cube, I was lowered in and sealed away in moments.

Cleaner and brighter than anything similar back on earth, it wasn't too depressing at first. It was all a milky white plastic with a clean, thick and clear gel pad for a bed. I had rented smaller places in Japan and Hong Kong years ago.

Recessed in the ceiling was a two way vidscreen monitor where I could be watched or communicated with if needed. Most times it displayed tranquil footage of places which were out of reach to an inmate or the harmless rehabilitative programs designed to instill guilt and remorse into the soul of the most career oriented criminal.

For the sleeping interval, the bright plastic walls faded to a deep blue. I turned away from the water basin/commode unit, silenced the vidscreen and tried to nap but the quiet absence of stimuli left me thinking about Strobos and the Sabian sisters.

Laying there silent, it occurred to me that I was probably responsible for Strobos getting away. If I hadn't gone to him with the news after the police first interviewed me, he wouldn't have been warned, wouldn't have known how close the investigation of Juliana's disappearance was getting to him. He must have gone into hiding right after I'd left.

It actually seemed he was working at the SleepCenter. He was monitoring the sleepers, looking at their data, running tests on their blood and vital stats. There was no way I could've guessed he'd killed the real phlebotomist and had taken his place illegitimately. The SleepCenter was attached to the spa facility recently. Accommodations for 40 sleepers were maintained automatically but there was always a staff of specialists attached to the unit to watch over them incase of emergency. Most of the clientele were recovering from extensive surgery or awaiting the transplant of cloned organs or limbs.

Strobos had seemed so sad to hear the bad news about Juliana. Even as I lay there in the holding cell, I couldn't help but entertain fleeting fantasies revolving around the idea that it was all a mistake, just a matter of a flaky spoiled heiresses or faulty employment records.

Later in the night, I even manufactured a dream wherein Strobos called or showed up to clear me, announcing he and Juliana were secretly wed. In this dream, Anastasia came forward with a video clip of the ceremony at a Chinese orbiting casino or on a tanker in the Arctic Circle after eloping quite miraculously from the moon. Finally, a deeper more merciful and dreamless slumber passed over me.

It must have been getting closer to the hour when they thought the inmates should be waking up, because the plastic walls of the cell were cycling through sunrise orange, pink and yellow. The screen above me brightened and the glowing greenish face of Basil Rathbone appeared to look at me.

"Goodmorning, Mr. Greysmith. We were able to pinpoint your location during the cruise up here. You have been cleared of any wrongdoing with respect to the death of Norbert Kates, however Anastasia Sabian doesn't corroborate your statement regarding the party you call *Strobos*, thus your remand continues."

"What do you mean? She knows him better than anyone. If he's in hiding somewhere in this complex, I'll bet he is in the Sabian suite, in the very lap of luxury while I rot in this white box!"

"You have been in custody for eleven hours, twenty six minutes," the 'bot said in response.

"Don't you see? He's gotten to her. She's probably afraid to turn him in. If he did kill Kates and maybe Juliana, he could kill her too, while you waste your time on me!"

"If such statements turn out to be truth, you may still be held responsible for interfering with the Sabian family's semisens. It has not been decided if you will be held responsible financially. You will be billed for the damage you caused at the beeGarden," it informed me.

"Please. Check into it. Anastasia Sabian must be hiding him. Talk to the staff at Crater. They've seen us all, they must know him. What about fingerprints and other DNA material?" There must be something at the SleepCenter in the phlebotomy lab. I've seen him in there."

"The area was swept twice but didn't turn up any stranger's prints or DNA material. We did find your prints and Norbert Kates' DNA. The Kates' DNA shows us that the lab hadn't been cleaned in sometime. As you are aware, Kates never made it back from his last recreation pass. I will interview staff and review security video from the Crater Club," It told me.

"And Anastasia?" I mentioned.

"I will interview her personally, later today. Enjoy your morning food service." With a blip it was gone then replaced abruptly by another live video feed. It was the other cop with the hip facial hair.

"Kates was killed by being robbed of his blood. He was a phlebotomist; a blood specialist. You pop up here with accusations about a phlebotomist who doesn't exist in any of our records. It's kooky as hell. Expect to be with us for a while," he said smugly then also blipped away.

*BLOOD WORKER FOUND BLOODLESS.* I could envision the clever boldface headlines. Things were getting complicated. It was a bit freaky but so was every other thing up here. I had nothing to do with Norbert Kates. The robot I damaged was another story.

The Sabian family semisens had flown in the day after Anastasia heard I was being questioned about her sister's disappearance. I suspected it wasn't just sent to protect the remaining sister. Many corporations and wealthy families used the semisens 'bots to track people down, to do strong arm work, lean on people. Vendettas were not out of the question, despite what futurists like Asimov wrote a century ago on the uses of robotics against people, their handlers would always find a way to override or disable the human safety programming.

There have been stories of 'bots breaking hands or severing fingers with customized steely claws. I wasn't about to be mutilated by a robot or indirectly by an impotent old jerk operating one from afar.

Seeing the glowing green skull scan the bar at the Crater Club then settle on me, I knew it was reporting back to its handlers. It had just froze there awaiting instructions, or perhaps it was shifting into *possessed mode* so it could be controlled remotely in real time. I wasn't staying to find out. I got away but not before it could get a fix on me.

They were outfitted with sensitive gear which took bio readings from several subjects near their target and could focus on something unique to follow; an irregular heartbeat or exceptionally low body temperature.

My first impulse was to let it follow me to the Sabian suite in hopes that Anastasia would shut it down or get it to leave me alone. Just the idea that it wasn't by her side was enough to lead me to believe I was in danger of someone using the 'bot to intimidate me, retaliate or take the law in their own hands.

When I reached their threshold, Anastasia politely let me in. She had actually put her arms around me, held me tightly for a few moments. I guessed her sister's disappearance had her shook up, left her emotionally raw and I was still a friendly face. It seemed a little odd with her family security 'bot coming after me. Maybe it hadn't been her idea. It gave me the impression that she didn't believe I was responsible for whatever happened to Juliana. She seemed so different, I actually forgot about the 'bot for a few minutes, which was just long enough for it to catch up with me, despite its particular limp.

The door to the suite slid open and the 'bot entered. "Adam Greysmith, conceived in Hartford, Connecticut, United States 34 years ago?" It confirmed.

"Obviously."

"You are being apprehended for illegal entry. This is Sabian family property," it droned.

"I know where I am. Anastasia just let me in," I said pointing to her.

"Where is she now?" It asked.

"She's right in front of you, you junk heap," I said as she stood there smiling broadly. The 'bot approached.

"You will be detained until jurisdictional law enforcement arrives. I am in communication with the authorities. Where is Anastasia Sabian?" It asked coming after me.

"Say something. Stop it!" I demanded as Anastasia fought hard not to giggle. Even though she was a few feet from the semisens it failed to detect her presence.

I wasn't waiting around to be mangled by a malfunctioning robot. I took off my leg weights, tossed them at the thing then leapt over and passed it to the open door. I was originally headed for my apartment in the employee wing but knew the 'bot had my address. There was only one place where I'd be hard to corner.

The earth was a sparkling slim blue green crescent over the greenHouse. Scattered couples picnic'd in the grassy common near the beeGarden. I casually strolled to the beeGarden's entrance and slipped inside when I was certain no one saw me.

Tremendous, the lunar bees hovered playfully above rows of genetically engineered orchards. The bees grew to the size of lemons up here. Maybe it was the gravity. Not being a scientist, I didn't know why.

Hundreds of these monster bees congregated about the hive, their collective buzz sounding more like chanting monks than insects. It was very peaceful. I sat at the tables set up at the concession and watched the slender robotic handlers harvest the raw opaque honey.

I knew it was only a matter of time before the Sabian's semisens caught up to me with its bio fix tracking gear. It was hard to stay cool despite the tranquil surroundings. I did what any frightened citizen would do. I called the police and hoped they would get to me first.

I could tell them about the malfunctioning machine on the loose before any real trouble started.

When I saw the semisens crossing the common, I didn't know whether it was the one attached to the police department at the complex or the Sabian unit.

The head displayed the two dimensional face of one of its operators instead of the normal grim and greenish hologram skull. It paused then started off in my direction without appearing to actually see me, betraying use of a bio fix. I had to move fast. I climbed up through the protective netting and slowly moved towards the hive, hoping there was another exit back there somewhere.

Up until that moment, I had never known I was afraid of the lunar bees, had never been close enough to see their formidable stringers.

"Adam Greysmith!" bellowed an old frustrated voice over the 'bot's audio system. I could see it trying to negotiate the net.

Several bees swarmed around my head making me very nervous.

It seemed there wasn't another way in or out of the beeGarden or if there had been I was too distracted by the big bugs and the 'bot ripping its way through the safety netting to come after me.

I took an empty tray from one of the robot bee handlers and it paused, trying to understand. I started to wave it around my head to keep the bees away, careful not to swat one. I had no idea what they could or would do if provoked.

The Sabian's semisen had closed in. It was no longer *possessed* by anyone. The green ghoul face was back on. Perhaps they didn't want to see what their 'bot would do to me or didn't want to be responsible.

"Where is Anastasia Sabian?" it asked, in the standard monotone.

"I left her with you, you retarded hunk of junk!" I answered while swinging at the bees with the tray until I struck a couple.

"You will accompany me to the police for further inquiry," it demanded as I swatted a few more bees carelessly. Suddenly there was a change in the tone of their buzzing. It had become loud and discordant, menacing. As a dark cloud collected and swooped towards me, I took refuge behind the 'bot before it could lock a steel cuff around my arm.

The big semisens was being pelted loudly as it swiveled around to get at me. I grabbed the nearest robot bee keeper; a slim, meter tall plastic machine and swung it ineffectively at the head of the Sabian's semisens. The beeKeeper came apart in my hands and said,

"Tut tut, it look's like rain. Tut tut, it looks like rain."

That's when I felt the first bee sting, right through two layers of clothing. I screamed and leapt forward, toppling the Sabian's robot.

Its head cracked on a length of irrigation piping which broke open, flooded then shorted out the 'bot's inner electronics. The loud pops, sparks and smoke scared the bees into retreat. I'd ran for the net in time to be met by the police.

Near the sealed door above me, a small round panel started to descend. It must be the food service they told me about earlier. Suspended by a telescoping plastic beam were two foggy soft cylinders. One was warm sweet tea in the top compartment and cool water in the bottom. The other held warm vegetable soup in the top section and long chewy strips of lightly seasoned tofu over brown rice. It wasn't too different from the food served at the staff cafeteria. It was probably whatever was left over. I ate and watched soothing footage of free people hang gliding over the Adirondacks.

The quiet stillness of the afternoon was deafening, it seemed that after my senses desperately sought stimuli, my ears cranked to maximum gain. The silence became an almost palpable squall of white noise.

Perhaps nothingness was the real punishment if you couldn't tolerate the insipid video programming they offered as rehabilitation. The stench, fear, filth, strategy, sex and violence of traditional prison systems must have proven too stimulating a lifestyle to be true punishment for those who chose to live with the same elements when they were free.

I watched an instructional program about carving canoes from tree trunks then dozed listening to a Mandarin lesson. I woke to Detective Lowe beeping out a goofy pattern on intercom to get my attention. Had known it was him, I would have feigned slumber. "What's the news, Lowe? You and your 'bot brother figure this out yet?" I asked, hiding my genuine anticipation.

"To complicate matters, Anastasia Sabian cannot be reached for questioning. More foul play may not bode well for your predicament," he told me.

"When you say *cannot be reached*, what do you mean exactly?"

"By electronic means and by an attempt to contact her at the Sabian suite," he answered, obviously curious.

"Who went there? Was it you or the 'bot?" I asked, wondering if Anastasia had found a way to become invisible to semisens robots.

"Inspector DDF43 went. Why?" Lowe asked.

"I'm not quite certain yet."

"DDF43 and two other semisens are going to attempt simulating a biofix from her medical records and start scanning the facilty," he said.

"I think you should go check out her suite yourself. The last time I saw Anastasia, her family semisens was on my trail, as you know. *It* couldn't detect her. I don't think it came after me because of Juliana, per se but because it couldn't locate and protect the remaining sister… Anastasia. I'm just putting this together now as we speak."

"I'll share this with inspector DDF. This is getting strange," he said smirking contentedly.

"Lowe, I'm cooperating, trying to help. I'm just waiting this out. I'm not guilty of anything. Could you do me a favor?" I asked. In the monitor overhead, I watched him arch his eyebrows curiously, in an exaggerated fashion.

"Could you get me a few vodka gels?" I asked hopefully.

"I'll see what I can do," he said quickly and blipped away leaving me with aerial footage of red robed monks meditating at the rim of a Polynesian volcano.

Hours later, there were two loud but non menacing tones. Near the middle of the floor, a panel opened and a small exercise unit rose from within. It could be pedaled or raised and adjusted for upper body resistance training as well.

I hopped on and pedaled for a while before resigning back to the padded shelf which served as the bed then dozed watching the programs for the day.

At some point, the food service disk had been lowered into my cell. I noticed it while tossing and turning. I spotted something silvery on the food disk, a squarish foil pack. Inside there were two different flavor martini-gels.

"Thank you, Detective Lowe," I'd said aloud. Spirits buoyed, I savored each while watching a program featuring a scantily clad female scientist who had decided to spend two months in the ocean with the last six blue whales on earth.

Intoxicated by the time the walls were fading to blue, I ate my food cold, lowered the sound on the video screen and tried to get some real rest.

I don't know how long I had been out, but I woke to a familiar voice. Immediately, my eyes went to the screen overhead, but it was silently displaying space walk footage from the previous century.

"I'm here, in the dark," Strobos said. There was movement in front of the dim plastic wall. It was odd, almost as if I wasn't looking at a silhouette but a shadow. The video screen above should have thrown some light on him, but he remained a black shifting shape.

"What are you doing here? Do you have any idea what I'm going through?" I demanded of him.

"I just want you to know that I never hurt Juliana. I know you didn't hurt her either," he told me.

"How the hell are you in here anyway?" I got up and reached out but connected with nothing. "What is this? Some kind of projection?" I asked, having become more curious than anything.

"Stay away from me. I don't think it would serve anyone well otherwise," Strobos warned.

"Just give me an idea of what's going on or I'll call for the guards or police 'bots or whatever!" I threatened, my hand on the intercom. He laughed at me.

"It's called sibling rivalry," Strobos had pronounced slowly.

"What? What!" I repeated. There was nothing. I got up and slipped on an empty foil pack from the martini-gels.

Winded, I remained on the floor a few moments and looked around. There was no one. The dead negative white noise was maddening. I picked myself up, raised the volume on the overhead screen to hear murmurs in Japanese over fading stills of plum blossoms in the air and rainbow scaled fish darting around in clear water over smooth stones.

My head throbbed dully as I wondered if the visit was my imagination or an alcohol amplified fantasy of wishful thinking.

Back up on the sleeping pad, I passed out until the walls were white again.

I woke when a mysterious part of my brain became aware of the screen above going suddenly silent. I rubbed my eyes and focused on it.

"Rise and shine, Partygirl." The 'bot must have been nearby or Detective Lowe simply enjoyed entertaining himself. I refrained from the crass retort I could have offered, recalling the liquor gels.

"So, am I free?" I asked, stunned by how timid my voice had become after a mere 20 hours or so of confinement.

"DDF43 will release you. It's his investigation. You will be released on your own recognizance," he said.

"What was it? Did you find him? Did something happen?"

"Neither. We just don't have enough to go on. The more we look, the less we know. It's all very inconclusive," he said grinning wildly.

"Did you check out Anastasia Sabian?" I asked, curious.

"She's a freak, and I'm not sure it's in a good way," he said, winking both eyes in rapid succession.

"So you saw her! Did the 'bot go, uh DDF whatever?" I asked him.

"We switched details. DDF43 interviewed staff at Crater, and I handled the heiress, why? What are you getting at? What do you know?"

"I don't know. Maybe I'm going crazy. The whole moon thing. Don't get me wrong, I do like it up here but sometimes it makes you a little introspective, too receptive to the imagination in the absence of the ten thousand things which made up a typical earth moment," I'd said almost thinking aloud.

"Deep, Grasshopper but what does that mean?" he asked. Lowe disappeared from the screen for a moment then returned, lighting up a dark clove cigarette. He sat puffing on it a bit, seemingly gathering his thoughts before speaking again.

"Anastasia Sabian made a move on me," he said uneasily. I just stared at him. He went on in detail.

"First, she just isn't my type. When I asked her about her sister, she casually mentioned that she's seen her. She wasn't concerned. It had no significance to her, and like I said earlier, she's a freak. I think she was on something. I reported everything to DDF34. I've seen a thing or two up here but not like her. The whites of her eyes were completely red, and I'm not just talking bloodshot. My eyes are bloodshot twice a week. The whites of her eyes were completely evil red. She grabbed my wrist," he said then took a drag and raised his sleeve and held out a the length of his nearly translucent moon pale arm, splotched with black and green bruising.

"Her hand was cold as ice and her grip, it felt like she could have snapped my hand off like an old piece of plastic." He saw me smirk a bit in the monitor.

"It isn't funny. I know most of my muscle mass is gone from being up here but I'm serious. It was inhuman. If we hadn't been interrupted, I don't know what would have happened," Lowe said seriously, perhaps for the first time.

"Interrupted by who?" I asked.

"I don't know. Her profile didn't mention a jawbone implant phone, but it seemed someone or something was in touch with her or had signaled her somehow then she threw me out."

"Interesting," I responded.

"I told everything to the inspector but you know they don't totally get the unspoken part of interactions. You know these people. What are you thinking?" Lowe asked puffing more clove.

"Anastasia was right in front of me and her family semisens, the one I broke in the beeGarden, malfunctioned or something.

Not only did it not recognize her, it didn't even register her presence. That's why I thought you needed to go see her instead of sending another 'bot. Now, I'm thinking it would have been better if you were both there so you could see if it was just their semisens malfunctioning or if she is somehow invisible to a 'bot's bio sensor gear. What you just said, "*inhuman*" is interesting. Maybe her bio readings are not in the normal range, maybe she isn't reading as human," I suggested, thinking out loud. "What could that mean?" Lowe asked, perking up to his own phone implant's signal. "DDF43 is on its way. He's coming to release you," he said.

In my mind, I had always envisioned the moon as a dusty place, a useless orb of gray grit, pock marked by eons of stray debris in its path. It always struck me as odd that nothing ever collected dust at the complex. Returning to my small apartment, to its dust free surfaces and the imperturbable plush pile of the synthetic carpet, always bothered me. Time didn't seem to elapse here, nothing would wear out. The kitchen and bathroom units were self cleaning. No matter how purposefully I would scatter my personal effects around, I couldn't conquer the clean, cold institutional fortitude of the space. My walls had those panels that changed color, like the ones in the holding cell. I set it to random and turned it on for the first time.

I showered then opened a liquor gel. I gulped a glob and tossed another over my head and watched it linger at apogee for that extra moon moment then caught it in my mouth, felt it dissolve cooly over my tongue then smoothly burn down my throat.

It was hours before I could decide what to do. On the one hand, there was the idea of taking up where life left off, back before Strobos, back before the Sabian sisters. Free, I imagined I would remain so, simply by staying away from all of them and minding my own business.

On the other hand was Juliana. I'd wooed her just a month ago but was feeling remotely ambivalent.

I had to admit to myself, in spite of the idea she may have suffered or even perished, there was relief.

She had been a beauty I admired from afar even as we'd shared a social circle.

After her watchful sister was distracted by Strobos, I finally had my chance to spend time with her. No matter how much I liked the prospects of a future with her, I knew it wouldn't have worked out for us, not in the long run.

I just couldn't back out. People were starting to know who I was. The staff at Crater knew my name and what I wanted.

The Sabians introduced me to one of the big Thump composers from China. I'd been on a quite a ride and didn't want to get off. In another month or so, I probably would have appeared on tabloid websites and had my fifteen minutes of fame. I might have been able to parlay it into a few interior decorating gigs in Vietnam or DuBai.

It had really become quite a sad affair the more I examined it. As I considered the remaining liquor gels in my fridge, I listened to a new Thump recording made from a rapid humming bird heart beat, blue whale mating calls and a chorus of various owl hoots.

I began to feel pangs of guilt, began wondering if any of this would have happened had I not introduced Strobos to the Sabians. Thinking further, I began to wonder what had happened. Where was Strobos?

There was almost no way to get off the moon without dealing with the government or the upper echelons of the multinational corporations that owned everything.

He must be here somewhere, despite what the police 'bot thinks. The Sabian family semisens couldn't see Anastasia, so it was possible that she was invisible to it somehow. Perhaps whatever facilitates her invisibility comes from Strobos, some chemical or device which has helped him to disappear from the lunar complex. Maybe, whatever trick he is using also allowed for the mysterious visit to my cell.

I squeezed the liquor tube out entirely above my head, let the long wiggly column of flavored vodka liquify and slither down my throat. No one ever talks about the booze buzz up here. There was never any mention officially or in any web brochure for the lunar complex.

Intoxication came much easier and it was different, it was more physical, made you more comfortable in the moon's lower gravity. Drunks commonly shed their leg weights, tumbled and swam around in the dimly lit corridors that stretched out away from the wing of the complex housing the recCenter, bars and clubs.

Guilt stopped me from swallowing a third tube, but not for long. I was slightly drunk and went out looking for something, answers or revenge, I just couldn't say which.

It was nearly terragrande or new moon when we were invisible to the earth bound because no sunlight fell upon us. Fleetingly, I hoped not to miss earthrise in the greenHouse but felt I had to act, if not for Juliana, for my own peace of mind.

I tried to contact Anastasia but got no answer from her suite so I decided to go in person. The last time I was there, things did go awry, yet she hadn't seemed unfriendly to me. I couldn't make any sense of what Detective Lowe said about her so I didn't dwell on it.

The door to her suite was slightly ajar, ominously ajar. No one's door anywhere on the complex malfunctioned and when it did, it was immediately taken care of by the maintenance crew.

The doors normally slide open as a response to a quick bio reading which has to match a record of one of the occupants or a number of registered guests. From the inside, they responded the same way or by voice command, recognizing a primary user. The door to the Sabian suite was open about an inch.

As fate would have it, I have installed a number of these myself and knew how to release the lock. The unit didn't respond, it must have been pried or forced open. When it was safe to do so, I wedged my foot in and pried it open enough to get inside. The lights were low. It was in complete disarray. "Stazi?" I called out uncertainly. I walked around a bit. It seemed empty. I called the police and asked for Detective Lowe. Before he answered a huge silvery orb came floating into the room from deeper in the suite. I had no idea what it was. It didn't look dangerous, but I didn't want to find out. Maybe it was a new type of security drone.

I'd just broken into and illegally entered the Sabian suite.

"Anastasia!" I yelled. The last thing I needed was to be found in the trashed suite of missing people just after bing released as a suspect, so I fled and the orb pursued. I squeezed out through the door, bounded down the corridor while looking over my shoulder in mid air. The orb was stuck in the door but I could see that it was flexible enough to get through soon.

Bouncing rapidly down the escalator to a common area, I thought I might be able to loose it in the maze of shops and automated dispensaries. I slowed down and took stock. Apparently, it did not follow me.

Darkness was creeping over the complex and people were taking refuge in the recCenter to spend the time drinking, exercising or absorbing media. The corridors were becoming deserted.

As sobriety crept into my consciousness, I found it necessary to have another drink to bolster my confidence.

Naturally, I headed for the Crater Club. In the darkness of terragrande the club's lighting was a multi hued strobe effect I usually found annoying.

It was one of the reasons I usually passed this time in the greenHouse. The club was also quite crowded.

I squeezed passed tourists to the narrow bar, a polished slab of giant sequoia. I made eye contact with one of the regular bartenders who nodded in return and served me a pair of my favorite vodka-tini gels. I immediately consumed half of the first one and turned to the writhing crowd of Thumpers on the sunken dance floor.

They were enjoying a new track from Shanghai. It was warm car purrs and whale calls, percussion supplied by what sounded like the syncopated heartbeats of a large mammal and its unborn fetus. It was brilliant.

Lifting the wiggling booze lozenge to finish the serving, I noticed someone looking back up at me from the dance floor. It was Anastasia, wearing the bioluminescent choker she liked for the dance clubs. She was caught in an undulating throng of young people who sought out the Thump scene with near religious fervor. They would leave home for years, dizzy on designer drug inhalants, liberated by contraceptive implants and funded by ancient relatives in medical stasis.

Before the track was over, it was full earthrise, darkness engulfed the moon. The club went black accordingly, stabbed with blue laser bursts.

For a moment, I could fix my eyes on her but in an instant she was gone. I slurped the remaining vodka-tini gel and made way for the exit. I was stopped by the 'bot with Basil Rathbone's sharply featured face.

"Greysmith," it called to me.

"I have to go, I think I can find Anastasia," I told it.

"We know. Detective Lowe informed me. I tracked you by the heavy metal tracers put in the food at the detention center. A standard practice. I also received information from one of the staff here at the club who said he saw Ms. Sabian here earlier. When I came and tried to get a bio fix on her, she didn't have one."

"What?"

"More precisely, the readings don't conform to human bio readings," it said.

"Meaning?" It didn't respond. "Well, if you can track me, I'm going after her," I said and rushed passed it to the exit. Having no real ideas of what to do if I actually caught up with her, I tried to open myself to everything instinctual.

The corridors were mostly empty, the maze of walkways between the clubs and spas were dark and complex. The intoxicated loitered and groped each other in the shadows.

Dark Moon Cult members solemnly marched chanting oblique dirges while waving rods of burning incense and amber laser torches. Their helium lined cloaks billowed spookily with each step in the low moon gravity. They were weird, but mostly harmless.

I followed their little fragrant parade for several minutes, hoping I'd come up with a plan of action. Maybe Anastasia was going back to her suite, I was headed in the right direction so it seemed like a rational place to start.

I heard a woman scream somewhere nearby. The Dark Moon people stopped and chattered amongst themselves. I went in the direction they were all looking. Around the corner, a figure stumbled and collapsed.

"Help me, someone!" I heard her call out frighteningly. I ran to her. In the weak gravity, she was bleeding in big red globs which rolled down her arms and shoulders from a deep slash in her neck. Blood on the moon always freaked me out. It took me a few moments to break away from her to use an emergency commScreen on the wall nearby I had spotted earlier.

When I returned, one of the more sensible cult members had lowered her cloak and was attempting to stop the poor woman's blood from rolling away down the corridor by pressuring the wound with her scarf.

The injured woman was conscious and held the young cult member's arm in a white knuckled grip that looked quite uncomfortable.

"The medics will be here any moment, and so will the police," I said recalling the heavy metal in my blood they were tracking me with.

"What's your name?" the cultist asked her.

"Chana Lesser. I'm from New York," the bleeding woman said and then burst into tears. The other cultists, having overcome their apprehension, now circled 'round and started to chant quietly, really getting something out of the event.

Norbert Kates came to mind, looking at the rolling blood.

"What happened to you?" I asked as delicately as possible. Serious violence always caught us off guard up here. The woman started to shake.

"She's going into shock!" the young cultist exclaimed, astonished. I crouched down beside the bleeding woman and she grabbed my arm.

"I trusted someone," she said, quietly shivering.

"She's got the chills. She's going into shock and then die!" the cultist gasped.

"Chana, you're going to be alright despite what she thinks. The medics are on their way and they will take care of everything, get you fixed up. They've all kinds of new techniques. You'll be fine. Could you just give me an idea of what happened? Who did you trust?" I asked.

"I had met her last month at an Inner Goddess Body Class. We had good contact. It seemed she understood everything, like she was just so beyond it all, you know. I thought we'd rub and cuddle, I'm not one of those, I promise you..." she broke into sobs and the cultists started to chant louder, annoying me to no end. I could hear the medic alert coming from somewhere close. "Was it Anastasia Sabian?" I asked, getting to the point.

"Yes, Anastasia," she moaned sadly, becoming paler every moment. The medics came racing down the hall on a robot powered electric trike.

"You've got this, right?" I asked the young woman who was examining her ruined scarf. By the time she looked up from it and understood me, I was gone.

"*Yes, Anastasia,*" I heard the bleeding woman's response over and over in my head. Had Anastasia gone berserk in the wake of her sister's disappearance or had she caused it somehow? Did she have anything to do with Norbert Kates? More questions without answers. What did Strobos do to the Sabian sisters?

We were the only new elements in their lives, as far as I knew. I had no answers, just crazy ideas, suspicions and meaningless connections. I could only follow the trail of blood. Having abandoned the route to the Sabian suite, I went in the direction of the SleepCenter where Strobos had told me he worked as a phlebotomist, where Norbert Kates would have been working if he lived longer. If Anastasia was on a rampage she might have the sense not to go back to her rooms.

Seeing the SleepCenter door had been pried open, I was certainly on to something. Heart pounding away in my chest, I quietly pulled the door panels apart enough for me to squeeze in.

The entry was dark. From somewhere deeper inside, I could hear Strobos playing his small alto sax in long wailing tones punctuated by short discordant bursts of notes.

"Strobos!" I called out. He didn't answer, just kept playing. "The police are tracking me. They'll be here any minute," I warned. I walked into the lab where the sleepers hibernated, where I had seen him before.

The lights were low, the sleep capsules, in rows of eight were illuminated by the twinkling status monitors on each unit.

I walked towards a translucent examination cubicle where the music was coming from and someone leapt from the darkness. I felt bare feet on my back then went crashing down to the floor, knocking over a small cart, scattering various medical paraphernalia.

A smallish foot on my back pinned me with such force it felt as if the owner could crush me with it.

"It's Adam, he must have followed me from the club," Anastasia said from above, foot still firmly on the center of my back.

"Stazi, what's wrong with you?" It felt for a moment as if she considered squashing me right there on the floor like an insect. "Stazi, please."

She took her foot off me and dropped down on the floor inches from my face, crimson smeared all over her chin. She must have been bloody from attacking that poor woman I found in the corridor and shed anything too soiled. All that remained of the outfit she had on earlier was the glowing choker and a skimpy black ribbed leotard. I rolled over and sat up.

"Why do expect mercy form me? You chased Juliana like everyone else. I don't know what she saw in a half queer little interior decorator like you!" Fast and feral, she took the upper lobe of my ear in her mouth and pierced it with her canines. In a moment the pain hit. I tried to swat her away but she grabbed my hand and pinned it behind my back. The whole side of my face hurt from the bite, as her cold tongue lapped my blood. I tried again to get her off me but it was a mistake. I screamed like an animal when she broke two of my fingers. To shut me up, she kicked me hard enough to break my last rib.

As I lay there holding my mangled hand and rocking slightly like a suffering child, she straddled me.

Stazi bit at my ear again to get fresh blood flowing. Trapped under her arms and thighs, she seemed heavy as lead.

Cold breath and tongue at my painful ear, she really seemed to enjoy herself, squeezing me as if it would cause my wound to bleed faster.

"Anastasia" I heard Strobos call out, his voice strangely disembodied as it was in my visitation a night ago, "A police semisens is just outside. I shouldn't be disturbed at this point. Stop playing with Adam. I am almost where I need to be," he told her.

There was a robot voice in the corridor. I never thought I'd be relieved to hear a semisens calling my name and couldn't help but feel gratitude for the industrious Japanese the moment it pulled the damaged door open and limped into the room.

"Adam Greysmith, you must not interfere. This is a crime scene," the 'bot said.

Anastasia let me go and leapt through the air.

"It's Anastasia Sabian, and she's fucking nuts!" I warned but it was too late.

Effortlessly, she took the protesting robot apart and carelessly tossed the cheap chrome coated components around the room until all that remained of Inspector DDF43 was a one legged heap of junk twitching around in a circle on the floor.

While she'd been distracted with destruction, I crawled to the translucent cubicle expecting to see Strobos.

Once again, he was a black shifting shape, this time sitting in a lotus position atop one of the sleeper's capsules. I heard Anastasia's crazy bare feet padding towards me in the low gravity, probably ready to leap and pounce.

I couldn't move fast enough to avoid her completely. The impact pushed me across the room causing me to fall into Strobos, who apparently wasn't there.

Falling through the black shifting shape, I was lost and grasping in star strewn space. I could hear voices but didn't understand.

It seemed somehow I came to rest or was no longer falling but floating, oddly buoyant in a warm body of liquid. As my eyes adjusted, I sought the surface and horizon of this impossible ocean. The stars above were bright blazing streaks of color across the sky. In what was perceptible as my first safe moment, I decided to assess my injuries.

Lifting my swollen hand to my face to try seeing it more clearly in the bright starlight, I realized the wet black warmth that held me was really the dense deep crimson of blood. It looked like an endless ocean of blood.

When an arm reached out, grabbed my shoulder and pulled me under, I thought it was death itself.

In the next instant, my eyes found light. I was back in the examination cubicle at the SleepCenter in a hibernation capsule with Strobos. He had opened the top and was perched on the thick plastic lid covered in blood. I jumped out and slipped in the blood and fell.

Anastasia, face covered in my blood, cackled wickedly. My hand and ear were both throbbing. I had no idea what to do and could only hope when she tore the police 'bot apart an alarm went off and help was on its way before the freaks killed me.

"How very malapropos," Strobos stated quite flatly, the whites of his eyes even more scarlet than Anastasia's.

"What?"

"My opportunity to undo what's transpired here has sadly passed," he told me.

"What the hell is going on here! We're soaked in blood! Have you lost your minds?"

"Perhaps she has," Strobos said as Anastasia started to feed from the blood filled sleep capsule like a pig at the trough.

"That blood is nearly useless now," he told her as he yanked her from it," I'll need the blood of three more sleepers to make another go at it."

"Is that why you're here? Is that why you guys killed Norbert Kates? I asked wishing I was wearing an audio transmitter instead carrying heavy metal traces in my digestive tract.

"Mr. Kates. He was an unfortunate, however very deliberate victim. There is so much at stake, so many wrongs to right," he'd said. I could tell he was hoping I would see things in a more positive light, despite the circumstance.

"There is no way I can really explain the Wall of Blood to you but you experienced it a moment ago. I can only tell you what I know.

The energy in living blood is the same energy which has coursed through and will course through the universe forever.

Through that blood someone like me can touch other moments in the past or future. Living blood is the link to eternity," Strobos said, notes of awe in his voice while Anastasia stood beside him absorbing the info as well, licking her abnormally huge canines which seemed to make my ear swell and sting more intensely somehow.

"You've been consuming the sick people's blood hibernating here? Do you have any idea how much money they paid for this?" I asked them incredulously, only realizing how meaningless the words were to the vampire nuts upon speaking them aloud.

"Inspector DDF?" came a voice from the partially opened door up at the front of the lab.

"That's Detective Lowe," I said.

"I'm in here. Fall back while it's possible. Summon reinforcements!" the damaged 'bot commanded from an indiscernible position.

Anastasia scurried around looking to silence what was left of it. I approached Strobos. "My hand is killing me. What do you think you're doing here? I've partied with the best of them but this scene is off the charts.

Frankly, I'm a little disappointed. I thought we were supposed to be friends. You've got this...Well, I don't even know what to call your problem but it looks like you took the two best looking women on this rock with you. You lied about your job, you're taking baths in other people's blood, you got her drinking it!" I ranted delirious with pain. "Consider yourself fortunate that Anastasia hasn't killed you. That's a good sign," Strobos said.

"A good sign? A good sign of what? That she and I skip the whole hand holding phase and go straight to the altar? Fuck her! She's crazy," I went on.

"Yes, perhaps she was always disturbed. She might have killed her sister with or without my interaction," Strobos said regretfully. "What?" I asked, unable to understand anything.

Anastasia found the 'bot's head. It still seemed to be functioning. The greenish Basil Rathbone looked around then fixed on me.

"Greysmith. I should have known you were trouble," it said reproachfully.

"Can't you see them or sense them?" I asked.

"I have re-calibrated several times. I can only detect a shifting darkness," it said.

"Can you detect my injuries? Take a bio fix on me. I'm sure the numbers reflect physical and emotional duress. I'm practically a prisoner," I said as Anastasia dropped the head near me.

"That cop left but he'll be back with more," she said, her toe toying with the glowing 'bot's head on the floor.

Strobos cleaned his face with a wad of paper towels, staring into the unknown.

"I may have missed my chance here. There may not be another opportunity," he said.

"I can detect...entities," the glowing 'bot's head emitted spookily.

"Silence that thing," Strobos told Anastasia who kicked it across the room where it hit the far wall then exploded in a cloud of sparks, glass and silicone micro beads. "What do we do with Adam?" she asked, sitting down on me heavily. Strobos looked at me for a moment.

"Do what you like. We must leave," he said and stooped over the nearest lab sink to clean himself off more thoroughly.

"Hey! Haven't I been through enough?" I asked, looking up at Anastasia, hoping they'd spare me for some reason.

"Strobos! Don't let her do this man! Maybe I can help you somehow," I pleaded.

Anastasia laughed maniacally, straddled me and started to lick at the blood rolling in little globs from my ear down my neck. A shot rang out. She froze for a moment then toppled over. Strobos became a streak of darkness above my head. There was a high pitched scream. I got up on my hands and knees to try crawling away.

Strobos had disarmed Detective Lowe by actually breaking his arm. He must have fainted when he saw the bone poke out of his sleeve and lay in the globs of blood on the floor like a broken doll.

Another shot hit the cubicle, inches away from me. There must have been a few other cops slowly moving in on us.

"Dion, they shot me, " Anastasia moaned, rubbing her shoulder.

"Yes, they're through playing around with us, there's an officer down. Just give up!" I yelled, trying to reason with them.

Anastasia reached out to me. The bullet must have knocked some sense into her.

"I need you now, Adam," she said meekly. I carefully put my arms around her as more shots were fired.

"We give up! Don't shoot!" I screamed as she bit me and started to drink my blood. I was dizzy but I held her still, struck by the sudden soothing warmth passing between us.

She seemed to recover almost immediately, threw me aside then practically flew across the room. I could hear the sounds of a brief yet horrible skirmish, then silence.

I was bleeding from a new wound under my collarbone. It was not a bad as I expected. I guess she didn't hit a major blood vessel. I could hear another siren in the distance, but it was suddenly quiet in the SleepCenter.

I got up and found the paper towels, fashioned a rudimentary dressing and looked around.

It seemed that Strobos and Stazi were gone. Weak and throbbing with pain and confusion, I staggered out to view the carnage.

There was an arm on the floor, several fallen figures and one man who didn't appear to have his head.

I fought back some vomit but then let it spray nastily through my fingers. I didn't want to see any more law enforcement just yet, alive or dead. The corridor outside was empty but the sirens were getting closer. I wanted to get as far away as possible.

I wanted a shower and a numbing number of drinks. Professional medical assistance might also be a good thing to pursue.

Something flashed up ahead. It was the silvery orb bouncing aggressively off the walls and ceiling, coming in my direction.

I scrambled to get away but not fast enough, it nearly knocked me down, bounded high above then paused before continuing on in the direction of the SleepCenter.

It must have been a remote surveillance drone. If it belonged to the police, they already saw me so I relaxed a bit.

I recalled the way the evening began, me and a few liquor gels. I was torn between putting it all behind me and trying to find out what happened to Juliana, poor Juliana.

I sighed heavily then reluctantly gazed at my injured hand. If only I'd passed this earthrise in the greenHouse with an audiobook getting slowly wasted watching the wisps of white cloud dance and curl over the Pacific, the incident could have been avoided.

Perhaps, taking a break from the situation would have let me face it more carefully.

Approaching a main intersection, I began to worry about what I must have looked like, covered in blood and puke.

Before any further consideration, I saw the orb coming my way again. This time it had projected a small metal talon. In its grasp was a familiar little alto sax. It passed so close I fell to the floor, certain to be out of its way. It went up high above the scant throngs of people going home for the night. I watched it rise high above the open square, probably on its way up to the solarium which was alway empty at terragrande in the darkness of earth's shadow. It became a silver speck then disappeared just before I passed out.

*8*

# THE WALL OF BLOOD
## 2050

I t was sometime after four thirty in the morning, I no longer wore a watch, for I can feel every single tick of eternity with an almost painful certainty. It was raining heavily despite the sun threatening to rise upon the horizon like a murky crimson welt on this beaten planet on the outer rim of this wounded system.

Didn't know why I kept returning to this solemn mortal moment, caught in a downpour crouching amongst the charred and random planks of a burnt down pillbox near the Pacific. Waves endlessly crashed at the steep rocky coastline below. I could remain in this spot forever if it weren't for mornings. Soaked in my best leathers, I could skulk to the shore and threaten myself to feel the light.

I travel, lone and freely from instant to instant, to the soft blurs in between. No one known to Golgaban or the Council of Others has the ability I was reborn with, so they try to keep me close.

Able to travel without the Wall of Blood made me intrinsic to Golgaban's reign. Of all the abilities that were possible to attain when one crossed over, mine was the least heard of.

Many of the Sang Gang; the deadly throng of carny, circus and biker types who brought me into the life had heard rumors of the Wall of Blood from Strobos.

He had passed through our little group bringing us tales of the great immortals like Golgaban. He tutored us in old world traditions culled from his centuries in Europe. Most importantly to me, he knew of travel to other points along the flat plane of conscious experience.

The others treated my travels as dreams or magnificent boasts because I had no additional special abilities at all. Aside from immortality and the daylight dilemma, I am bound by commonplace physical laws, most disappointingly; gravity.

While so many reveled in dances above the forests and glassy frozen lakes, I would watch from beside the campfire or haunt the rough trails of hikers looking to feed upon the wayward, intoxicated or lost.

My physical form, helpless and inert during this mind travel, I'd only indulged for brief periods. Often, I would push myself to points in the past or near future. I'd stroll up and down through foggy metropolitan nights in cities like San Francisco, New York, Boston, Shanghai, Paris. Bathed in lights and sound, I'd absorb the details of urban life that were missing from my rural Rhode Island youth.

Strobos believed me, for he had travelled but relied on the Wall of Blood or a similar living blood portal to enable him. Also vulnerable while traveling, he often relied on the protection of a Familiar. Most often, Strobos stayed close to a woman he was in the process of bringing over to Vampirism to see if she would become stable enough to be a companion.

Distantly, I became aware of a signal, an alert sensor I had set up in my chambers to warn me of someone's approach while traveling. I had to let go of the stormy Pacific and return.

The binary red dwarf stars that warmed this dead rocky satellite were slipping behind the gas giant we revolved around which bathed the Blood Moon in a brief infrared twilight every other night. Awash in a the crazy part of the spectrum only faintly visible to our kind, I was still fascinated by it after the thirty plus years spent serving Golgaban.

As habit dictated, I reached for the edges of my Iron Age replica coffin and felt the smooth recesses worn there by aeons of habit, or so I had been told when it was sold to me.

Golgaban's crypt was genuine Iron Age, worn and polished by his touch over the centuries. Many Iron Age items were now popular with Vampires of position here and *Elsewhere.*

Man may have first smelted ore and fashioned the first casts on earth yet it had been we immortals that had a genuine love for it.

Metal weaponry was not as dangerous to us as the wooden arrows, spears and stakes of early civilization. Not only did it represent the era where we began to truly taste the immortality which allowed us to flourish, it was when we could begin to own items that would endure the relentlessly cruel tests of time.

In the glass globe of glowing micro organisms framed in crudely fashioned iron serving as a monitor, a member of the Council of Others appeared and summoned me to the dais where we met with Golgaban. Recently the only topic of discussion was Strobos. Over the last 20 years he'd become obsessed with the idea of undoing things in the past he considered mistakes.

He originally sought out the Wall of Blood and time travel for going back to save his beloved Demetra. Unfortunately, I believe it is not possible or at least improbable in the strict mathematical sense. What he wanted involved undoing the deeds of others. For reasons I don't understand, the deeds of others involved so many different strands of possibilities that undoing one moment didn't always produce the future one desired. Only undoing your own deeds, with clear knowledge of your own intentions seemed to be effective. When it didn't work out, you were not always in the position to know if anyone else was effected.

Strobos believed undoing his own deeds in the past would help him better understand how to undo the deeds of others.

He would construct his own crude life-blood portals, immerse himself in fresh blood to go back in time and undo some of his kills.

That was when the trouble began. Sometimes he would take back the moment he turned someone into a vampire, thereby undoing hundreds or thousands of human deaths. This caused upheavals of large segments of people and even changed small strands of history.

Golgaban was only concerned with the Vampires. I myself, was brought over by someone Strobos had turned; Drucilla of the Sang Gang. If he took back the moment he turned Drucilla, I and a large number of the Sang Gang would cease to exist if their human lifespans had elapsed or go back to being human if there was still time.

I put my velvet cape on over my leathers and went to attend the meeting.

The dais was resplendent, a cross of modern technological majesty and the brutality of crudely smelted Iron Age metals which was all the rage with the immortal in crowd.

A huge panoramic window looked out upon the Wall of Blood where the largest animals were sacrificed above to maintain a crimson curtain of life-blood a vampire could use to cross time and space.

At the center of the raised dais a long polished iron conference table was attended by Golgaban at its head and flanked by the ever changing Council of Others.

Nearest to Golgaban was my chair. I was respected to some degree because of my position, yet there were skeptics among the Council who doubted my ability despite my presence at the table.

The chatter in a dozen tongues ceased when Golgaban raised his hand. Truly one of the ancient and pure vampires, he is a fearsome sight to any of us who had been human once and maintained our appearance as such.

Smooth pale gray was his flesh, his huge skull crisscrossed with throbbing veins, reptilian eyes aglow with fresh life blood. Beneath his heavily draped cloak was a tail that could thrash a man in half.

Legends of vampiric origin indicate the first vampires found earth at the time when the dinosaurs ruled and roamed. The massive beasts were herded for slaughter at the Wall of Blood, which was a key cause in their extinction just like the larger blood bearing beasts of this now dead system.

Awareness of the span of Golgaban's reign was staggering, left most awestruck. I had to admit being one of them. Golgaban had been amongst the very first landing party on earth, had the first taste of Brontosaur blood and knew what he could do with it.

Recently schooled in the language of the ancient ones, I didn't really get the details and would be briefed later on, but the general sense was alarm. Strobos had succeeded in reversing some of his actions from 18 years ago that created a member of the Sang Gang, who had in turn begat five other vampires. This shifted the hierarchy of the group. The resulting infighting claimed the destinies of two others who in turn had made eight other of the Sang Gang's current number.

I found myself shaken. I was a direct descendant of Drucilla, who had once vied for leadership of the New

England gang. As she was one of the most dangerous and reckless types, mingling his blood with hers was an action Strobos could never reconcile. If he decided to go after her and succeed, I would return to earth a frail old man, destitute and alone.

Drucilla's physical whereabouts were not known, only that she languished in the Sixth Void and was of no danger to anyone. Now, it seemed my safety relied on her remaining there.

Golgaban took a vote although no one would dare challenge his decision.

Strobos must be stopped. No one on the Council of Others had any pity for a vampire who killed vampires. To rob a mortal of his lifespan was cruel, to take eternity from any being was almost unthinkable if you looked at it that way. An almost perfunctory vote was taken. It was more a show of support for Golgaban than a real decision making process.

I found myself timidly raising my hand despite sharing Strobo's opinion on reckless unnecessary violence and a disregard for discretion at a time where mankind possessed the technology to detect, roundup and defeat many of the less powerful types on earth.

The only thing which remained undecided was who would take on the task of stopping Strobos? There weren't many on earth who could match his skill and knowledge and the one's on earth who rivaled him were not bound by the council. For many, the existence of the original race and the Blood Moon were folklore. They were creatures of a modern society in an isolated system and in many cases, unaware even of each other unless they were related by blood and the fang.

Strobos was not to be destroyed, which made the task seem even the more improbable. Destroying him would only destroy vampires that he turned, which was the reason he had to be stopped. They wanted him captured, disabled. Exiled to the Sixth Void, where he could no longer do anything to anyone.

Currently, among the Council Others there were only three humanoids who could even venture undetected on earth and two of them had let their appearances go centuries earlier in order to fit in on the Blood Moon.

Suddenly, I realized a silence and the collection of huge crimson eyes focusing on me. It was decided that I would be the first wave of action.

I would have to use my rare ability for travel, which many doubted anyway. It would be a way of proving myself before the Council.

Even as I argued, the Others rose in turn from their seats and wished me luck. Aside from being able to travel mentally though time and space, I had no other powers to speak of, yet it didn't seem to matter to anyone.

Alone with Golgaban, he told me I would do well to find an ally, an earthbound vampire whom I could turn against Strobos to help achieve the council's objectives. Best would be a strong vampire that would be threatened by his activities as of late and turned into our champion. It would be no easy task. Locating vampires on earth always presented difficulty. Turning them against each other was another matter entirely.

Aglow with bright red neon, I stood above the bustling thoroughfare of Commonwealth Avenue in Boston. The Citgo sign blazed brightly behind me, merely a petrol industry trademark but a landmark beyond meaning in the area.

Down below, I sought a trace that would lead me back to the Sang Gang. 1986 was just before I would have been known to them, perhaps the best way to be of influence. As I had no impressive physical powers, perhaps by knowing their fates, I could appear omnipotent and gain influence.

I closed my eyes and refocused my presence. Not as exciting as flying but safer than actually being there in the flesh, I opened my eyes again strolling down Kenmore Square some hundred meters or so below without actually leaving my chamber on the Blood Moon light years away.

There was a club in Kenmore Square called the Rathskeller which was popular with the Sang Gang. It was an edgy feeling multi level bar where they could hang out, listen to loud rock music and meet likely victims amongst the clubs patrons.

The club had been a haven for punks and goths alike whose style and ideals would make almost any member of the Sang Gang appealing. I showed my old ID and paid the entry cover just for the fun of it, got my wrist stamped and went downstairs.

Traveling this way, I was more than a ghost but less than a vampire. No one was really sure how I did this without the Wall of Blood.

A group of girls was on the stage stomping to something between ska and punk that was dark and catchy. Throngs of black clad twenty year olds swayed and bounced accordingly.

Not an immortal in sight. I smiled at a girl who was looking at me and then disappeared.

I could pop up on the perimeter of their lair by the shore in South Boston but wondered if one of them might sense me the way they would if I were actually there.

Maybe it made no difference. I needed to make contact but needed to get someone alone to really be of influence.

I had the advantage. It was the Sang Gang's least stable, least organized era. Drucilla was vying for leadership with Ivan, who eventually took over after Strobos left Drucilla.

Drucilla and Ivan had competed by giving into the gang's wilder instincts for aggression and excitement with a recklessness Strobos couldn't tolerate.

Drucilla would be ideal but her future would lead her somehow to the Sixth Void, rendering her eventually useless.

Upon a shore strewn with boulders and broken stone lions that seemed more suitable roaring at the foot of an old library, I huddled and listened to the the purr and wail of motorcycles in the distance. The Sang Gang was close. First in sight was Phipps.

His Harley hog gurgled and sputtered as he stopped. He was a fat black bald bastard with no sense of humor, yet was always laughing at something.

I didn't know who had brought him over, and no one spoke up if anyone had ever asked. Strobos had joked about Phipps eating the vampire who'd made him. Phipps hadn't laughed at all. Maybe he was a candidate for my mission.

Next were the Kluska twins, two ruthless dimwitted Polish girls Drucilla had made one night. They were originally meant for blood slaughter, but

Drucilla needed easily manipulated confederates in her attempt to usurp Ivan.

Next was Timothy, a local biker and one of Ivan's first wave. He was meaningless now, as he was or will be destroyed in the recent upheaval brought on by Strobos's tampering with the past. I toyed with the idea of trying to capture Strobos at this time, long before he even thought about undoing things but had no idea how.

Phipps started the fire as the others parked their cycles. Ivan showed up and circled, kicking up sand, wildly making his entrance as usual. He stood on his bike as it slowed and remained standing as it spun around to a soft landing in the damp sand closer to the surf.

Gordon, a tall lanky vampire from somewhere further south, tossed gasoline on the fire causing it to burst and rise in a plume just in time to fully illuminate Ivan.

Bearded and vividly tattooed, he strode up to the group and put his arms around the Kluska twins and took a invigorating squeeze of both their asses as they nuzzled his ears.

"Lets party! He roared and slapped Phipps' bald head after breaking the embrace with the twins. Phipps started boiling eggs over the fire while Gordon tuned in a college radio station playing an old group called The Fall on his bike's custom stereo system.

Vullo, came next on his trike, he was one of Drucilla's. She must be close. He had the two unlucky guests of the evening riding with him. Wide eyed and young mid western students, they were clearly one of Drucilla's offerings. She was always trying to impress

Ivan's group in order to win their alliance.

I started to remember the evening and cringed. Vullo looked like a Vampire should, black haired, thin and pale. Dressed in black with a frilly old light green vintage tux shirt from the 1970's.

He dismounted then walked up to Ivan and did the Sang Gang greeting. Face to face they grasped each other on the top of the left shoulder with the right hand and smirked, bumping foreheads.

He introduced the night's guests as Troy and Melody. They were Boston College freshmen Drucilla found on Landsdowne Street trying to get into a club called Spit with fake ID's.

Just then, Drucilla rode up to the fire with me, my arms still clinging to her waist even after the bike stopped. When who I had been took his helmet off, I could see something was odd about him. She could see it also. "What's wrong?" she asked in a whisper as everyone was busy introducing themselves to the night's guests who were holding each other's hands and almost quivering like lab bunnies awaiting the next test.

He stood there holding my helmet, staring off into the darkness. He could see me somehow. Who I'd been, saw who I am.

When he found my eyes in the darkness, I disappeared.

I opened my eyes at home in my chamber, safe in my coffin on the Blood Moon. I lay panting for a moment and closed my eyes again. When I opened them again, I was he, who I had been, Drucilla shaking me. I dropped the helmet.

"Where were you?" she asked.

"I don't know," I said. I couldn't tell whether I had taken his place or became him or was inhabiting his or my old space somehow or if he was just out of sight for a moment.

You were doing your mind thing weren't you?" she asked.

"I'm not sure what I'm doing, did, done," I answered honestly.

I had no idea this would happen. I'd thought I would just see myself, observe and interact at will. It seemed, that in my presence, I had no choice other than to be myself upon mutual awareness.

Exasperated by what she couldn't comprehend as usual, Drucilla sneered at me a bit.

"Go over and sit by Phipps. Get ready to feed."

The fire roared and popped, the music blared and laughter ensued as antics were performed by nearly all to entertain and lull the evening's prey in to pleasant compliance.

Troy was sitting by the fire being cheered on by the group as he started making out with the Kluska twins. His hands on more nipples than ever before, he was insensitive to his hometown sweetheart's pleas, quips and eventual whimpers.

Gordon was trying to comfort Melody by blowing smoke rings and forcing tiny plumes out of his ears, but she wouldn't look away from her beau. Gordon always knew how to impress a girl. Before becoming a vampire, he was the type of guy who would ignite his farts on the first date and used to sit around reminiscing about the look on a girl's face at the sight of his most memorable stink bursts, most often perpetrated in the dark of movie theaters or the romantic intimacy of the Drive-In.

Vullo was more successful, he led the girl away to stroll by the shoreline and brushed away her tears.

The gang started to clap in time with the radio as the Kluska twins striped and danced around the young man, who was obviously a bit bashful, his pale skin blood-blush red in the firelight, an embarrassing lump in his green corduroys.

With a few fast yanks and rips, he was in his tube socks and blinded by his shirt. Drucilla was holding him now, whispering taunts hot enough to distract him from the situation. He felt six slender hands probing his body, feeling his young firm fleshiness for the most blood filled first bite that wouldn't be too harmful to take right away.

On her knees, one blonde twin started to lick and lap at his inner thighs and scrotum. He began to relax and enjoy himself, his hands guiding her head between his legs as Drucilla played with his perking nipples and the other twin kissed his back and raked her ragged nails across his ass.

When Troy's penis found its way into a cold mouth, the twin behind him bit his fleshy triceps as he screamed from under his shirt. They pulled him to his knees and Drucilla bit his ear as he struggled. Above it all, Phipp's full laughter bellowed. With an old rusty sickle, Gordon opened the boy's back in a wide gash and started to catch the blood in a bowl of pealed hard boiled eggs. He shook them around to coat them in the warm fresh blood and passed the seasoned treats around.

Shakily, I ate my egg just as I had back then.

They let the boy loose. In the first moments, he didn't know whether to run or let the Kluska twin continue blowing him. Phipps laughed at his indecision, trembling like a happy big black Buddha in the firelight.

At the moment she felt his orgasm, the twin bit down as he screamed pain and pleasure over the applause of the group, the crimson saltiness spurting into her mouth and running down her chin until she gagged then belched. Steadying himself, he tried to flee and take the shirt off his head at the same time. Again, Gordon struck with the blade opening the back of Troy's right thigh just in time for Vullo to return with Melody who froze and couldn't scream. Vullo had eaten the tongue right out of her mouth in a kiss then passed the girl to Ivan who locked his lips on hers not to waste any of her blood as she struggled. He then pealed her shirt off, popped her breasts out of her bra and molested the young frantic woman as she fought uselessly in his arms making awful sounds.

Gordon was catching Troy's blood in little paper cups then passing the warm shots around. There was no use in watching the rest of this again but I wondered what would happen when I returned to my time.

Would my past self be sitting there stunned and changed by my presence enough to make Drucilla wonder what was going on.

Would who I had been, say anything about the incident?

Upon recalling Drucilla's irrelevance in the present, I opened my eyes nevertheless and let the balance of that particular evening remain a memory.

I climbed from my coffin, stretched and paced. Going back there made me realize, why Strobos was out to stop some of us. The hunger we felt wasn't always just for living blood. Immortal, we could grow bored and from that boredom often grew malaise. It wasn't only the insane one's who practically lost their minds in the crossover. I wondered about my mission, wondered if an ally suited my methods. It was one thing to convince someone to join a cause but it didn't mean that individual could be controlled.

I wandered over to the window. They were a wild luxury of the Blood Moon. Polarized and over a meter thick, they allowed us to view our rising and setting binary dwarves as they slipped behind the planet we revolved around. The nearest of the two stars had just past behind the gas giant which was our mother planet. A faint and filtered impressionistic glow of actual starlight crept across the room. It made me remember the day-suits Strobos had told me about years ago. A day-suit allowed a vampire to safely take brief late afternoon trips into the daylight world.

The suits were not perfect for every situation. They were best used in big cities were the streets and alleyways were narrow. These areas were often older parts of cities wherein the facades of buildings often threw deep dark shadows and a day-suited vampire might step out into the dim shafts of light for several minutes in foggy or cloudy weather. A vampire in an early day-suit, before the innovations of smoked and tinted or polarized glass, often would see and take in sunlight.

If you examined ancient armor for battle, the suits which most efficiently covered the body and the face were used as the first day- suits.

It was not unusual for a vampire to have reddened, sunburned eyelids from head gear that allowed him to see more than form or shadow. The more crafty creatures would tie lightly dampened cloth around their eyes for some protection while allowing them to do battle and interact with in daylight for brief periods.

It has been said that a human vampire who takes in too much sunlight regains a reverence for their race. I often imagined being caught up once again in the bright cadence of sunshine and shadow, of basking in the pure beauty of sun kissed scenic vistas and felt the tale could hold some truth to it however foolishly romantic it sounded.

Nothing was impossible, given all of eternity.

Myths of astounding bravery and heroism have often rose around such beings. There was the legendary El Cid, reputed for riding into battle dead. A nobleman exiled for suspicion of murder in Spain, he was called back into battle against the Moors because of his astounding prowess on the battlefield. Europeans have conflicting accounts surrounding the petit Joan of Arc; an armored warrior for whose supernatural and superhuman sacrifice is also renown the world over. Perhaps these were tales of vampires who have felt something warm in the light of their nearest star. Suicide rates on earth were always highest in polar regions that undergo extended periods of darkness.

The sun isn't a god, merely another star twinkling in another's distance but the undeniable source of everything, the source of lives we feed upon but may never again enjoy.

We, as humans had our gods, erected our monuments, houses of worship and studied our cannons of catechism, yet lived by the movement and grace of the sun.

Everywhere on the Blood Mood you can find figurines of stars like the sun, giant iron obelisks representing the glory and horror of a brightly burning star. Amongst the sect of pure original vampires, they hold the same significance and bear the same awful majesty as representations of Satan or more appropriately Lucifer; luce or lucent, filled with brightness or light.

Perhaps Strobos had used his day-suit too many times. I wondered if he had one recently or how many day-suits he'd purchased in the last twenty years or so.

I searched through an iron strongbox which held my earth things for the stack of yellowed business cards from those days. There were some vampire friendly shops and businesses which were either immortal owned and operated or in most cases, the businesses of familiars or their relatives and descendants.

There was an antique shop in lower Manhattan just off Nassau Street in a narrow cobblestoned cluster of establishments closed to vehicular traffic which sold the best day-suits available on earth. It was run by a familiar, an old man whose father had become a vampire shortly after he had been born in the 1940's.

The hunger upon me, I left my chambers and strode to the dispensary at the base of the Wall of Blood.

The blood spilled for time travel was still good if one went down there early. Best to feed before taking another trip, even if it was only mental time travel, it left me feeling drained and a bit hungry having considered the wild feeding that had gone on back in those days.

I had my heavy flagon filled with warm frothy whale blood and drank half of it on my way back.

I couldn't help thinking about day-suits. Having been a somewhat of a mentor for me in the New England years, almost anything Strobos did seemed worthy enough to investigate and draw my own conclusions. Back in my chambers, I contemplated the thick luxury windows some of us had installed in the last decades. He wasn't the only vampire who took in starlight or sunlight. These windows give us a little taste of what we crave. Almost nothing is a greater temptation than complete destruction to the biologically immortal. As a human, I can recall the moments of dancing around with suicide in my heart, but knowing time was limited and death was eventual made it seem a hollow and even vain enterprise.

Perhaps a trip to New York was in order. To find and capture Strobos, I would have to understand him better. If I took in a little sunlight maybe it would give me better insight into his actions and motivations.

Maybe, I wanted to delay what could just turn out to be a very dangerous undertaking with an old friend.

Nassau Street emptied into the financial district. After five pm, the once bustling streets of commerce become lone and silent. After sunset it was a lower Manhattan ghost town.

Closed off to vehicular traffic, the cobblestoned lanes were lined with old shops and new. Pale light and sparse shadows in the windows of ancient facades lined the street. Some of the businesses looked like they'd been around since the 1940's, I thought, strolling past the haberdashery at the corner of Beekman.

I passed a very modern looking twenty first century establishment, a snooze bar. It was already closed for the day. I looked inside. They had a group of very modern nap capsules harried office types could sleep in at lunch time, science fiction style.

They made me think of coffins, nicer than the one I was in on the Blood Moon. They were curved and plastic and cozy looking inside. Designed for daytime rest, they would be ideal for any vampire. I made note of the shop for future reference. Plastic lasted for aeons, but didn't have the sentimental value placed upon Iron Age smelting so it probably wouldn't become trendy on the Blood Moon.

On Theatre Alley, I looked up at the address on the business card for Mann & Boehrer Antiquities. There was a light on. I stepped up to the door under a heavy stone portico and pressed the third in a row of dim buttons on the intercom unit.

Seconds later, there was a buzzing sound and the lock clacked. I crossed the polished marble, entered then closed the ornately patterned gate on an old style traction cage elevator to ascend.

The elevator opened into a dark corridor. Apparently stepping out onto the plush runner activated something. Narrow, but high ceilinged, it was lined with tall glass display cases whose lights flickered on in succession.

The first held an intricate looking antique microscope, lacquered brass still gleaming. The etched plate on the case credited the marvel to W. Watson & Sons of London, circa 1910.

The next held a trio of European broadswords, in the center, a 17th century Schiavona with a jeweled basket hilt. There were full suits of armor, the colorful O Yoroi of 5th century Samurai, and a greened bronze Dendra Panoply from Greece's Mycenean period. Before I had time to browse the last group of cases, a door slid open.

"Not quite the way I'd imagined our next encounter, Mr. Summertime," a familiar old voice greeted from the darkness.

"You can tell the difference so quickly?" I asked as Jurian Mann, a vampire's son, came forward and curiously laid his hand on my shoulder.

"There are subtle signs one learns to recognize over the years, Sir. Certain shifts upon arrival."

"You haven't changed in decades, Jurian," I remarked, looking past him into the shop, "this place, on the other hand, has definitely benefited from the new era."

He followed me in as I walked passed the twin rows of display cases, glass polished and gleaming. They held everything from weapons, watches and crown jewels, to esoterica and rare electronics. The warm wood tones and deep crimson carpeting were the same as they had been when I first visited in the 1980's, but the 21st century was evident almost everywhere.

A tremendous curved OLED monitor silently displayed news in one corner appointed with a leather sofa and a coffee table made from a huge Indian textile printing block.

On the table there was a silver platter, mixed matched china and an ancient looking samovar obviously full of something hot.

Perhaps I was interrupting my old friend's meal but it seemed he was expecting me. There was a cup, a charger and setting for another.

"Can you eat anything?" Jurian asked.

"I have. I don't know how it is for anyone else because I don't use the Wall of Blood for travel. What I do isn't quite understood yet."

"I imagine you are not here merely to browse or reminisce, not in that state, if you don't mind me saying so, Sir."

"You can drop the whole *Sir* thing. I was never that kind of guy. Makes me feel like you're trying to sell me shoes. I'm not in a big hurry. I'm somewhere safe, on both sides."

"But you are here for something. Word travels, even betwixt the stars."

"You're aware of the Council's decision regarding Dionysis Strobos?" I questioned, as I sat on the cool leather.

"I am afraid your findings here may not bode well for the shop, despite its history."

"You know something that Golgaban and the Others don't?"

"Is that not why you have come?" Jurian asked, confused apparently.

"I did come about Strobos. I was curious. I was wondering if perhaps he's been using day-suits." At this, Jurian relaxed his posture somewhat and allowed himself a chuckle or two.

"Not very recently, or if he has, he's using an older one. One he commissioned in the early 1990's."

"Do you have a picture of it or the pattern and plans. I'm especially interested in the headgear."

"I have a similar model from the same pattern. The differences are only minor technological enhancements." He stood for a moment and exhaled.

"There are roasted quail eggs in a reduced sanguineous glaze," he offered with an upturned palm indicating the samovar. I opened it and took a skewer of the small sticky eggs and followed him to the backroom.

Never having been in the backroom, I stood agape. The cavernous space didn't seem organized until I followed Jurian to its center. Everything was in rows radiating away from a big semicircular worktable cluttered with decades of various electronic and chemical projects, rare antiquities cased in wide glass cylinders, repair and restoration jobs. One row looked like items to be shipped, delivered or picked up.

Jurian sat at a high-backed office chair and swiveled away from me to face a group of monitors as I ate the small eggs.

I walked down the line of packages glancing at the addresses and was startled to hear something move. A two foot red claw snapped at me.

"Super fuckin' nova! That's the biggest lobster I've ever seen."

I heard the old man laugh at me.

"You've met Dutch. I am babysitting him for one of your number, a woman from the upper eastside. No one you know. One of the new breed," he explained, approaching. "Lobsters are biologically immortal and having no blood to drink they've become popular with some vampires here on earth and *Elsewhere.*"

"Nice," I laughed. "I never thought about it. Monsters with pets."

"I do believe they are kept more in the spirit of mascots. Dutch is almost 40 years old. He is the only one I've encountered with a name. I have that day-suit design up on the screen."

I stepped back to the center of the wild array of items surrounding me and pulled up a bench near the monitors.

Zooming in on the headpiece, the detail around the vision slit was interesting. The inside of the headpiece covered the wearer's eye with a built in goggle nearly an inch thick. It was composed of a stiff gauze folded like a Chinese fan or pressed in a honeycomb pattern.

"Do you have a headpiece I can try on?" He lead me down an aisle of cases to the day-suits.

When suits of armor faded from use on earth after the Middle Ages, Japanese Shinobi or Ninja uniforms were used, but impractical in daylight with the exception of overt acts of aggression. There were traditional looking black Shozoku uniforms hanging in a bright box lined with colorful Hokusai prints.

The best outfits were made for winter or cold weather use. They were heavy duty day-suits which would let a vampire trek full afternoons in inclement daytime weather when more layers of protection from the elements were normal.

The modern day-suit was two simple layers. A fitted unitard of completely opaque material was worn under what appeared to be a traditional trench coat lined with stiff panels of a photon repellent carbon.

The headpieces were more of the photon repellent fibers in the shapes of various regionally appropriate brimmed hats. The hat connected to a full head mask then was usually disguised further with big sunglasses and scarves. They were most effective in situations when rushing around without interaction was commonplace. You could blend in in any major city then dash around outdoors for brief periods in the late afternoon when the sun's rays were more directional and thereby easier to avoid.

Jurian opened the case with a key on his belt and stepped up on a plush green velvet stool. He detached the faceplate or mask of the headpiece and passed it to me.

Under the mask, I touched the stiff gauzy honeycombed lattice of the thick goggle.

Sensing my interest, Jurian opened a draw in the case and offered me an extra goggle insert to examine. I held it up to the light but couldn't really see through it at all.

Intuitively, the older man sensed my question before I could pose it.

"If you wanted more light, you simply pushed the pattern until the stiffened gauze was more flush, flattening it to a single layer of protective screening."

Pushing at the pattern with my finger, I could see more light by spreading the gauze out.

"So it really is flexible. You could expose yourself to as much light as you could tolerate."

"Exactly, Sir."

"Earlier, you were saying something about what I find here being trouble. Has Strobos been by the shop recently?" I asked, looking around the immediate area for anything that made me think of him.

"He comes often, bloodtripping mostly."

"Why?" I asked, feeling anxious all of a sudden.

"We have been working on something new," he explained, "something he said was certain to be of interest to *you*."

"Me? He hasn't seen or spoke to me in decades. If he's been using the Wall of Blood, I would have known."

"He doesn't need the Wall of Blood or the old blood bath basin," Jurian said as I stared at him almost incredulously.

"You mean he's found a way without a blood portal?"

"No?"

"I don't quite know what you mean, Jurian. You say he bloodtrips, right?"

"Many years ago, my father had tried fasting in order to spend a peaceful season with us. The lack of blood would eventually send him into fits of delirium, especially if he needed to be restrained. I would go to his rooms, play my viola for him. Sometimes spoon feed him a gruel my mother prepared of yolk and plasma to keep him going.

In those calm and coherent moments, he'd speak of his travels to the Blood Moon, of mighty Golgaban and all the things he'd seen *Elsewhere*. He told me of a vampire who knew how to bloodtrip, *fangs in her prey*." Jurian turned and motioned for me to follow him.

"I've heard something like that but I've never seen anyone actually do it. If you say Strobos has found the way, I have to believe it's possible."

"We've been developing a unit during his visits, a *bloodtripper*. I am afraid it may be the weapon he is using to facilitate this new mayhem. So you see, I have fear for the shop. If Golgaban or the Others on the council hear of this, there may be some rather awkward consequences, I'm afraid." He stopped at the end of the worktable in front of a few small pieces of gear that covered the user's face and ears almost completely. There was a rather obvious blood reservoir at the top.

"This bloodtripper works?" I asked looking at the other partially assembled models and parts.

"It is missing one part, a small cartridge slides in here," he explained, indicating a narrow slot at the back.

"What does the cartridge hold?"

"Strobos says it's a neuro compound, the secret behind the Wall of Blood."

"Secret?" I asked, curiosity peaked.

"When one goes to the Wall of Blood for travel, there is a small ceremonial procession."

"The old singing bowl they pass you to sip from is spiked with something then?"

"That is one way of putting it, Sir."

"Strobos says bloodtripping doesn't work for every vampire. The neuro-compound helps those who aren't naturally predisposed to the talent. He expects you understand more about it than anyone else."

"I don't know if that's true. I don't even know what he really means by that. The Council just wants me to confront him with the consequences of his recent doings and try to reason with him..."

"Know one thing. I am an old man. I can't claim to understand everything under the sun. They want

Strobos stopped. That, I am clear on," he told me and I interrupted. "They only want him *stopped*. The Sixth Void is what I was told. He's is to be detained indefinitely. Disabled somehow. We can't continue to..."

"Strobos bloodtrips *from* the future. If you intend to stop him, I don't believe success is imminent."

Jurian's words froze me in mid thought and I felt myself panicking light years away. "You'll have to excuse me, Jurian. Thanks for everything," I said and flickered from sight.

Waves endlessly crashed at the steep rocky coastline below as the Pacific came in to roar and burst away in spray. Looking back up at the small burned down structure silhouetted against the splotchy gray night sky, I saw movement and took cover immediately.

Hugging the algae slick stones, I approached but saw nothing. I sat and looked back at ocean, focused on the dim lines of foam rolling over the black water. In minutes, I was calm again.

If what Jurian told me was true, and Strobos had a future outside of the Sixth Void, it didn't necessarily mean Golgaban and the Council failed to stop him. It didn't mean I was in any danger, yet the distinct possibility seemed to linger in the air.

I walked along, my coat tails flapping loudly, my leathers damp in the spray. I pictured Drucilla's face, the curve of her fangs and the slight veiny marbling of her pale skin. I recalled our brusque courtship, becoming her Familiar and the nights we shared as she ushered me across the dark threshold, away from life and the living. If I focused on the moments of memory, they were dense with activity not frozen or static but vibrant, millions of particles in flux. I could pull myself through those particles, back in time but it hardly seemed necessary. Nothing involving Drucilla ever was.

She had lured a plump and freckled, busty blonde to a bar on the outskirts of Boston, a place in Allston ironically called The Livingroom. The lighting was sparse, the space appointed with lots of velvet cushioned sofas and loveseats. Flatscreens silently emitted sports events and old films while new wave throbbed. The room was dense with smoke, tobacco and the sweet curls of clove, skunk reefer.

The blonde pulled her sweater over her head and sat between us. There were spots of blood drying on her tight translucent top and her too tiny denim skirt. Her pale thick thighs and upper arms were splotched with the telltale bruising of being mishandled by several.

Drucilla had her thin arm over the woman's shoulder, a hand roughly grasping one of her huge breasts as she cozied up close to her on the cushions.

"She bleeds the richest blood, the blood that would be life," she tempted, parting the woman's thighs as she kissed her.

I never played much with any of my victims, especially if I planned to drink them to death, but there were moments when the submission and the raw desire of the host to please was so great, that I've given into perverse wrongness with the insatiable fervor of a late virgin.

I remembered burying my face in the insane tangle of her bright peroxide mane, my hand upon the smooth curve of her lower back as it arched and moved to the music and her fatal passion. I held her close enough to feel the cold jab of pain shoot through her body as my canines pierced her earlobe.

Drucilla's hand was lost up the blonde's skirt churning hot moans from her mouth as I kissed and sucked her lips. Blood on Drucilla's delicate fingers glistened darkly as she smeared it on my lips, pushed her fingers into my mouth.

Warm insanity in endless potentials, my mind was pulled to a near infinite array of temporal loci. Eyelids closed, my minds's eye gaped at faces in agony glaring from where they bobbed in the deep crimson tide of the Wall of Blood.

Drucilla had pulled me back into the moment, her sticky fingers clutching me as if she could have prevented my traveling. Her whispered words seemed meaningless at the time as I fed, frenzied by the taste of our victim.

"To drink of female blood is opening a channel to eternity. Blood is connected. Our immortal blood is one power, one entity we feed upon as it feeds upon us. One entity connected by our number. Slash at the wrist to share the bliss. Severe the arm, its digits desist."

"Severe the arm, its digits desist," I said aloud, finally back in my chamber from my favorite stretch of Pacific coastline.

She'd called our number; the ranks of the undead, *one entity*. I had never heard anything since about that so called *one entity*. It was, however, easy to see how connected we were. To destroy the vampire was to release his victims.

Over the aeons, we found a way to prevent this by drinking the blood of a different immortal thereby linking yourself to another's fate if whomsoever begat you was in danger. It was known as being *crossblood*. As it sometimes resulted in a switch of allegiances, it wasn't done often.

I thought of Drucilla in the horrible stasis of the Sixth Void, pictured her fury in being trapped.

If she was harmless, perhaps I was in no real danger. Unfortunately, it would be easier to stop the reckless hellions of the Sang Gang by destroying her, causing the leaves to fall from her twisted branch.

Standing before my window, I watched the line of shadow slowly creep back away from the dim impression of starlight visible through the infrared haze. If Strobos had taken in too much starlight, or sunlight, might he even consider his own deeds in an unfavorable light?

If Strobos is was or will be bloodtripping from the future, how far? Perhaps it meant he couldn't stop Drucilla or the Sang Gang in the current decade. Perhaps he found a way to stop them from sometime far in the future. I had no way of knowing anything without getting closer to him, but where and when? It made no sense to watch Jurian's shop. Strobos had been expecting me there. I ran my hand along the smooth cold iron of my coffin then reclined inside. Curled up in my densest velvet throw, I was ready for a brief reprieve.

It seemed like an infant at first, the proportions and loose lotus position. Its arm hoisted a huge and gleaming hammer-rattle then swung it for another reverberating strike that seemed to propel the tremendous ring of the gear I was riding on. The burly giant arm glistened with exertion, strike upon strike, bringing me closer to its horrible face and blunt contorted features.

Sharp teeth gnashed in giant golden gears, interlocking and rotating each other as I stared into the intricate clockworks below, dreading each futile and repeated tick. Alert, daymares departing, I sat up and stretched.

I gazed over at the living swarm inside the view monitor and spoke the command to tune in on the daily broadcast from the Wall of Blood. It was a view to the sacrifice of hundreds of creatures for the daily fresh flow.

I was in time to see 20 or 30 eight foot tall gelatinous looking eyeball creatures herded over the slaughter trellis where micro fine pulses of wide vertical laser bursts sheared their bodies apart. In another gruesome instant their remains are pressed by a counterbalance weight of previous carcasses.

The odd species was first found on an interplanetary blood expedition and was paraded about the public square outside

Golgaban's fortress. Their method of locomotion had intrigued me at the time. These big eye ball creatures secreted a gelatinous substance in the shape of a ramp they would slide down, re-absorb and repeat. They could see, travel, consume food and water by membrane contact. They lead entirely intellectual existences for the most part. Useless as servants, slaves or soldiers, blood was their only value.

The next appeared to be a group of mammals abducted from a remote latitude back on earth, at least I thought so. They were jackalopes or something, prancing and looking around one second, then falling in bloody heaps after the laser flash.

If Strobos was so adamant in his efforts to stop senseless violence, how could he tolerate the Wall of Blood? Obviously, he couldn't stand against the Council of Others or Golgoban but it made me wonder. It made me think of the time after he left the Sang Gang and began destroying the vampires he had turned if they'd become beasts prone to reckless mayhem. Focusing my energy on the details I knew such as the time of year, the region, names of places and points of interest readied me. Closing my eyes and opening my mind, I traveled once more to New York.

The Sun had set a short time ago. Couples strolled arms akimbo, charmed by the old world architecture and variety of shops and pubs the Austin Street/ Ascan Avenue enclave in Queens afforded them.

Clad in my best leathers and a thick black sweater, I stood on the platform at Forest Hills station looking down over the colorful little intersection to find the building I wanted.

In another instant, I was within, peering around in the darkness. Machinery whirred and clicked in the tiny room. A reel of film had ended and bright white light funneled out of the projector into the theater below. I could make out the dark rows of empty seats lined up like plush pews in a modern synagogue or temple.

On the stage in harsh shadows, Strobos was down on one knee cradling a young woman covered in blood. Naked, her pale skin appeared nearly incandescent in the projector beam. On instinct, I willed myself into the theater below to slouch in the last row for a better view.

The young woman seemed conscious even though her head had been partially severed. She looked up into his eyes, seemed to beckon slightly with her lips. Her beauty held me agape for several moments, before I began to wonder if Strobos would sense my presence somehow. He held her close to kiss and stroked her sticky body from the crest of her sternum down to take gentle hold of her mons pubis as she bled out in his arms.

I opened my casket and sat for a moment in thought. It felt as if I'd encroached upon a very private event. The woman was obviously a new vampire, brought over by Strobos himself. A human would have been in no condition to communicate with its head hanging off. It seemed he may have had her consent in the destruction. I wondered what the Council would make of it. As long as he terminated new vampires with no bloodline to an other of our number, it didn't seem to be reason enough for the Council or Golgaban to take interest.

The situation need more investigation but I had no real clues on where or how to begin. I stepped from my casket and began to pace the stone floor. The Council of Others was mainly concerned with the Wall of Blood.

Thinking back to Jurian and his worries about the bloodtripping units, it was easy to connect the Wall of Blood with a portable device that allowed the user to travel in what seemed like the same manner. If it was perceived as a threat to the Wall or the regime, the topic should have been discussed and debated.

I could even see a connection from the Wall of Blood to my own special talent for travel.

I wasn't viewed as a threat on the Blood Moon, or was I?

The ancient Chinese master philosopher Sun Tsu always recommended that enemies be kept close. I was being kept quite close to Golgaban by the Council's recommendation as if I was a valuable asset, a strength of the regime yet at the same time most of the council harbors doubt about my ability.

Tired of pacing my chamber, I pulled my black and red cloak from the hook and slipped it over my head.

I walked the winding spiral of corridors that lead to the ground level of the fortress and out into the public square. Swarms of pale green glowing insects hovered and swooped, throwing their light randomly on the abstract maze of bleached bones fashioned from Wall of Blood remains.

Immortals strolled trading memories, browsed alien curio shops and blood pudding confectionaries.

I climbed up a short section of bleached white whale bones to a small and odd terrace in the maze sculpture I'd found decades ago in my first years on the Blood Moon.

I could look out to the dark horizon back at the spires of the fortress and watch the glowing swarms of insects brighten and fade as they broke formation like the slow ghosts of a lightning flash.

I lingered in that spot, trying not to think for a while, hoping something overlooked or significant would spring forth from the details and agenda of my mission, but it hadn't. I carefully went about climbing back down, wondering if I would ever possess the kind of insight that could let me make progress.

For an instant, I froze with the feeling of being observed. Slowly, I descended for stable footing while searching the darkness around me. A stream of glowing insects passed nearby, illuminating my inexplicable watcher. There, upon another crudely formed terrace of alien bone, was one of the huge eyeball creatures I saw slaughtered at the Wall of Blood this past sun down.

Somehow, quite inexplicably it hadn't been bled and destroyed.

Unblinking, the big creepy eye seemed to focus an energy on me and communicated visual information in what I could only describe as a telepathic manner.

First and most frighteningly, was Golgaban's face looming above me, disembodied and ten times its size, eyes burning red with fresh blood and power. A hot hellish gust rolled over his jagged discolored fangs and making me back away in sheer vertiginous peril. In his roar, there were alien words I've heard but never understood. Like a soap bubble, the vision burst away and was replaced by a most unexpectedly beautiful face.

Amidst the darkness and bone, only a few meters away from the huge viscous eyeball creature, a young woman's healthy and pleasant countenance hovered. As warm as any memory of sunshine I still clung to, deep in my once human soul, I was drawn to her eyes and smile.

Suddenly, she appeared to be speaking to someone. It was as if I was looking at a recording or memory. Before I could give her another moment's thought, she too was gone and replaced by Strobos. He looked weak, depleted of energies, physical and otherwise. While the vision lasted, I could see he was being restrained in some manner. When the image was gone, I felt a cool dampness on my face, perhaps even a stickiness. The eyeball being's communication wasn't telepathic.

An unseen duct sprayed me with a sensory excretion my body absorbed and interpreted. Curious, I slowly approached the big eye. I wondered what else it saw, what else it knew and why it was involved at all. Why did it know what I was involved in?

More than two meters tall and at least a meter wide in the middle, it focused on me and sprayed.

This time, the scene was like a reflection that seemed to overlay and fit into where we were. I could see myself and the alien, my hands making membrane contact with it, absorbing more information. I stepped from its gaze and stood near its left side just as in the vision.

It must be the future, I thought, and spread my hands out over the alien. I remembered a wetness, right before a jolt of static electricity which seemed to vibrate throughout my body from every fang and follicle.

Pulsing bands of multi hued brightness radiated from an inexplicable distance. On instinct, I stepped forward, miraculously penetrating the alien's animated gelatinous form completely.

In a welcoming warmth I, began to loose sense of self, of form. A cellular transference was taking place, neurons fired in a synchronous overture that lead to something I could only describe as orgasmic, freeing me from all tension and fears of ill will.

I started to have a sensation familiar to my own mind traveling and bloodtripping experiences, recalling that the strange beasts were being slaughtered for their living blood.

Looking up at the domed ceiling and the ornate lines of trefoil encircling it, I knew it was earth and immediately wondered about the time of day. Electronic music throbbed and pinged, encapsulating foreign dialogues in abstract consonance. It was clearly a recent year, but nowhere I could recognize. A fluid band of cool bouncing light radiated from a huge modern chandelier fixture in the center of the club. It was a huge tank flood lit from above. Inside, a tremendous immortal jellyfish seemed to dance to the music, bright red stomach aglow at its center, dozens of tentacles in soft gesticulations. Similar to the lobster I encountered at Jurian's, *turritopsis nutricula* was biologically immortal and a favorite mascot of the new wave of vampires on earth.

I didn't think they grew to be so huge. I recalled seeing them on sale in Japan but they were only a few millimeters wide. It must be a mutation or an engineered breed similar to the sad miniature horses we earthlings tampered with simply because we could.

Unlike the lobster, the immortal jellyfish journeys through eternity by transdifferentiation of its cells which allows it to get young and start over again.

The woman next to me wore a backless dress revealing her tattoo of a fist-like heart engulfed in star fire; a human with a vampire image from *Elsewhere.* I stood and turned, looking down on the dance floor and surrounding terraces of plush lounges and circular neon bars staffed by topless hosts and hostesses.

About to descend and circle the bars, I wondered where I actually was at the moment. Was I still on the Blood Moon experiencing the alien's sensory memory or bloodtripping in the alien's blood to another time and space? Before I could think of anything that would serve as an appropriate test of my circumstances, there was a silence. Somewhere in the cavernous club, a digital recording of a bell tower's sonorous clangs sounded the midnight hour. As the twelfth bell's tone decayed, a gong was struck somewhere below.

On the lowest level beyond the bars, I spotted the gong trembling near tall double doors that were being propped open as a queue of guests formed before it.

The woman next to me stood up and gazed down at the people lining up as she reached for her phone. I decided to test the boundaries.

"Please excuse me. I don't really come here often. As a matter of fact, I'm here for the first time tonight," I said as she looked over at me, trying to gauge my intentions.

"Who are you with?" she asked, possibly curious about which vampire I shared blood with.

"I just want to know what's going on downstairs," I answered.

"It's the Offerring. It's really 3aKat's main attraction.

"*Zawkat?*"

"3akat. It's *sunset* in Russian. The Sunset Club. Harlem South. Whoever you came with should have mentioned something about it," she said knitting her brow.

"I came here alone."

"Really," she said, eyes becoming wide with sudden delight. She put her arm on my shoulder then her fingertips found my neck. "It means, you feed for free. My name is Reese and I'm warm and wonderful," she whispered, her fingers moving from my neck to my lips. I realized she was looking to touch my fangs, another of eternity's psychophants hoping to mingle our bloods and cross over. Temptation was dizzying in her proximity. It has been a decade or longer since I've had consensual congress with a living woman or drank human blood. I wondered if I could possibly indulge myself. Unaware of my true physical circumstances, it might seem like a trespass if I was actually still inside another sentient entity.

"Take me down there," she said, already pulling me by the arm. Suddenly, I found her irresistible. We took a few more steps then spun around, arms linked, practically like dancers. I pulled her close to look at her eyes, the wide eyed wonder, the beauty and mystery that was woman. Then her warmth felt more like familiarity. She was the woman, the face shown to me as a vision before I ventured into the odd eyeball alien. Her hair and makeup was different but it was almost certainly the woman shown to me by the alien.

Perhaps we were meant to meet. She broke our embrace and turned to face the open doors below, where couples entered for what she called the Offering.

"What are they checking at the door?" I asked referring to the trio of burly bouncer types hovering about a small pushcart at the head of the queue.

"The short haircut, that's Misha Cherenko. This is his club. He is at bloodline's end here in the city."

I watched him greet his regulars and skeptically inspect others in the charming manner I've come to associate with the new wave of immortals on earth who treat Golgaban, the Council of Others and tales of *Elsewhere* as lore.

We descended further. At the last landing, the staircase and bannisters became a twisted forest of black wrought iron and the plush berber carpeting gave way to stone.

With candelabras burning, the lower level reminded me of the Cloisters further uptown or some wealthy swinger's sex dungeon.

Queueing up with the other patrons, a huge drum could be heard inside steadily beating out the seconds of anticipation. In front of us was a Goth couple, head to toe in black, black and dark ghoul-green nails and makeup. Behind me, a vampire joined the line alone. He was a tall thin creature with a pointy goatee and waxed mustache. I expected him to pull a monocle out of his breast pocket to further examine me.

I forgot about him as we took steps closer the the entrance and Reese squeezed my hand.

"I'm a bit nervous. I've never been down here before."

"I'm sure it will be a learning experience for us both," I said wondering how my presence would register to Misha and his crew. As impressive as

Misha's girth was, the men who flanked him didn't need to be the walking dead to intimidate me. They were broad backed bearded men each wearing a twinkling blue tooth headset at his left ear.

The twin headsets made me wonder if Misha was really in charge. I watched them screening the couple ahead of us. The woman giggled as the guy she was with paid an impressive amount of crisp colorful currency for the decadent spectacle of their evening.

I imagined the Offering, as Reese called it, was a *draining room* of sorts. Many successful vampires on earth and *Elsewhere,* maintain a room stocked with blood victims to eliminate the need for a hunt in the middle of the day or when it became inconvenient.

Ads were placed for seasoned kitchen staff, tender young nannies, bright tutors and sexy au pairs. Transient applicants were often "liquidated" on the spot. A draining room became a necessity if you entertained travelers who were feeling run down and depleted from a lengthy journey.

I wondered if the Goth couple understood what they were about to partake in was real and not an expensive bit of Hollywood show biz wizardry perpetrated by struggling actors. I wondered about the fate of any living being in a draining room feeding frenzy, paid customer or not.

Misha grabbed the Goth woman, smelled her hair and squeezed her ass hard. She was overly receptive and strutted proudly into the slaughterhouse.

I looked over at Reese, she was amazing. I didn't know how I was going to handle the screening. I saw the big bearded men look her over. One of them put his hand on Misha's shoulder and spoke something to him as he turned to look at me. *"Horrorshow, horrorshow!* You bring great fortune to the club tonight," he said quite obviously looking at Reese. The bigger men on bluetooth watched me much more intently.

Inside, the drum pulsed loudly. A magnificently nubile African woman in chrome body paint plucked melodies from an ornate cage of various sized chimes and bells while a huge primitive looking drum was beaten by a red cloaked dwarf with outrageous curving mutton chops framing his tiny wrinkled face.

Instead of bleeding nudes hanging from wrought iron hooks in a huge warehouse basement, it seemed they were going for something with a more sophisticated gallery appeal instead.

Couples wandered in a dark maze of curtains finding intimate spaces where victims sat on little fainting couches sipping steaming teas from angular modern china in dark violet crystal. Topless men and women, apparently first bite novices, milled about like zombies dispensing fresh towels and party favors.

Wide eyed with wild wonder, Reese wanted to explore, her confidence bolstered by the reception we'd received at the door. Almost amazed myself, I had practically forgotten about it.

Thinking about the big bluetoothed men, I looked over at Reese who was peeking around corners, thrilled to finally get into the club's privileged section.

Maybe they were waiting for her and didn't care who brought her in. There was a quality to her, something beyond sheer physical beauty and a heart free of fear. As I browsed the collection of bus station runaways, baffled tourists, babbling missionaries, lost seniors and random douchebags there were to choose from, Reese was infinitely more appealing.

A wave of anxiety rose in me when I couldn't see her any longer. I rushed about trying to keep my calm. I stumbled into a blood orgy. It wasn't Reese. A tall and tan California blonde, her faded denim in shreds, was beset upon by six vampires.

They had already groped, bled and fucked the life out of her. Belching and grunting in libidinous abandon, five still enjoyed hideous delights with the perfectly formed corpse. A long fanged female crouched on the floor chewing the stringy striated muscle of her heart, pale face half crimson from the feast.

In another curtained off corner, transexual immortals screwed each other while slurping the fresh blood of a uniformed football player from his jock cup while he dangled uselessly nearby from a harness of thick braided velvet cords knotted to resemble a huge spider's web.

There was a scream that gave me a start and I began to rush around searching. The dwarf seemed to be beating the drum faster. Eyes flitted about registering my dismay and then I found Reese.

A smile in her eyes, she sat contentedly, engrossed in conversation with a man I easily recognized by his beaten paratrooper boots. It was almost a relief to see Strobos in the mysterious depth I was swimming through.

His dark hair had an unfamiliar sheen to it. He was healthy looking. In the full flush of a blood rush, the whites of his eye were vivid scarlet. Gone was the forlorn creature in repose. His tux, definitely vintage, yet meticulously maintained, was worn over a dark sweater.

"Are you going to stare at me, Gary or say something profound," Strobos asked without turning away from Reese.

"If you've been expecting me, then you know why I'm here," I said.

"And *where* are you Gary Summertime?" Strobos asked.

"You're a vampire named Gary?" Reese commented.

"Gary is an old friend and welcome here anytime."

"You run this place? How could you? The day-suit and sunshine..."

"Yes, day-suits. Where's yours. I called down to the coatcheck girl. You didn't leave a day-suit with her and you didn't come up through the tunnel." Strobos challenged then leaned close to Reese and whispered to her.

"She's here with me," I said forcefully, suddenly feeling linked to Reese in the insane valor of standing together against insurmountable odds.

"I should have her right in front of you. Make her beg to suckle at my blood vessel for the myriad of infinity's fulfillments." Strobos took Reese's face in his hands, kissed her eyebrows.

*"Take this kiss upon the brow, and in parting from me now, this one thing I avow, you are not wrong who deem my days have been but a dream.*

*Is all that we see or seem but a dream within a dream?* Edgar Allan Poe, I am certain, found more than driftwood on the night's Plutonian shore. We are tuned into that blood frequency whose ministrations keep dead flesh vital, keep our number stark and fleet. We are connected by its current, connected by an eternal force older than life. I have learned these crazed catechisms in crowed catacombs. I have been singed in the half light of cities. I make no claim of a higher understanding, only that the inconsistencies in reality make it compelling enough for contemplation."

"A dream within..." I thought aloud as his attention shifted back to Reese.

"Dare you wish to see with forever's eyes. Rest your head on my shoulder, feel what is honest from the promise," Strobos ran his hand through her hair and gazed upon Reese's throat for her juicy jugular. I lunged at him and watched my arm pass completely through Strobos as he turned to smile at me. "Golgaban...he thinks," I said, still attempting to touch him.

"Ah yes, Golgoban our distant leader, our keeper, jailer of souls," he said as Reese stood and began to take her clothes off. Omnipotently alluring in the nude, she nearly eclipsed all concerns. We both paused. In more hushed tones, Strobos continued.

"I am here, Summertime, to stop *you*. This young woman," he said as her last underthing floated to the floor, "changes the balance if she takes immortal blood." A phone bleeped and he held up a forefinger to indicating his need for a moment. I stared at her tattoo trying to think.

"Let them in. Misha has an application on his phone that lets him take Bitcoin or VertCoin," Strobos finished and pocketed the small phone as the tall goateed vampire I saw earlier leapt upon Reese and sank his fangs into her smooth shoulder. Presumably the minor bite was intended to make her last longer or leave enough to share as another followed him.

She toppled in a slow moan as he took loud slurps of her blood.

"We will drain her until her heart beats no more and I will take her head and feed it to the murky bowels of the Atlantic," Strobos said as he stepped right through me. At that moment, I recalled the alien membrane, the visions of Reese, Golgaban and even Strobos. I must have been sprayed with a psychoactive excretion which polluted my blood. I couldn't help myself.

I grabbed at the tall vampire and he tried to back handed me but reeled in bewilderment when I could not be struck.

A bald stout mortal came in next and dropped his robe. Clad in leather and huge polished metal rings, he had probably paid a quite a bit for a kinky necro-romp.

Strobos drank from Reese's neck, then raised his face to her eyes and held her in his gaze for the final vibrance of her life.

Overcome with a mixture of fears and doubts, some mine others alien, I approached the gore huddle.

"Where are we, Strobos? New York or the Blood Moon?"

"I'm on a rooftop in Astoria at dawn, in the midst of a very interesting experiment," he said looking at the helpless young woman he had whispered to only moments ago.

"Never to see the sun, an eternal butcher on the hunt and on the run. I have spanned centuries while you have only served Golgaban for decades. I have, at times thought there were no vampires," he said, crossly eyeing the human who coated his engorged gonad in blood and took hold of Reese's legs while grinning with wretched mirth.

"I have long considered whether or not this is everlasting life or eternal damnation, that we perhaps scurry about deluded in the abyss," he explained then kicked the bondage clad death fucker hard enough to send him flying through the curtains to disappear with a complicated crashing.

"I have oftentimes felt this existence to be Hell and Golgaban our devil. Then something really complicated happens." He was gazing curiously at a corner of the dark curtained space as he spoke to me.

"What do you mean?"

"For one, your old flame is burning a path right for you. Drucilla is loose."

Upon hearing her name, a final nerve gave way inside me and I attempted to mind travel, but couldn't no matter how completely I could picture my rocky coastline, the pound and spray of surf. "She has already gotten to the Council of Others. The Sang Gang will attempt to usurp power at the Wall of Blood."

He closed his eyes took hold of Reese's hair then severed her head roughly with the edge of his old boot.

"Drucilla was behind the plan to get you back to earth, but it seems you have outsmarted her."

"What do you mean?"

"You. You are talking to me, a misty emanation from that alien over there. I cannot even be certain you exist any longer as a separate or independent being," he explained direly, Reese's dead head at his feet.

"But, but I…am here. I, she, before this…"

We both approached the huge creature as it watched us.

"I've seen others trapped and absorbed by their kind. Even if I tore it apart right now, your cells have been integrated with its cells. You, Gary, no longer exist in any practical way. If you are anything more than a trick of that creature's prowess, I hope it continues to see the benefit in projecting you long enough to aid our faction in the push for power at the Wall of Blood."

*General,*

*When a window high above the city is left open more than a few inches, or especially, if it's open almost completely and the curtains billow wildly in the wind, I don't stand any closer than I would to any natural precipice.*

*Whenever I have crossed the room and found myself bewitched by those same currents, gazing down at the herds of honking cabs, double parked delivery drones and the occasional clash of random fender benders involving automated vehicles with incompatible upgrades, the same trepidatious excitement of being poised upon a cliff high above a rocky coastline as waves crash and roar, ensues. Is it a cowardly fear of falling, or a fear of having the courage to attempt the irrational?*

*I have sought as so many others have, for more, to be aloft and embraced by those currents like the billowing curtains imbued with a life beyond their otherwise inert forms.*

*If I wonder, even for a moment, if I should recuse myself from further duty, does it mean I should continue? In recognizing thoughts that stray from the generally accepted views of reality and the human experience, does that recognition grant me further buoyancy to avoid the depths of my own entanglement?*

*I am certain, General, you find the tone and content of this mail to be inappropriate, yet feel it is my duty warn you that I fear becoming a man of divergent consciousness. It is a world and always will be a world in which flux is the unchanging dynamic.*

*Uncertainty is the constant in the equation of eternity. Is the very underpinning of common reality falling aside? Our planet is covered mostly in sea, certain only in its mysteriousness. New and amazing species of creatures are being discovered in the birthplace of life constantly. There is nothing to suggest that live does not still evolve in the deepest dimensions of its unseen darkness. Our scientists are beginning to understand the mechanics of invisibility and teleport matter. I recall a period when a host of possibly habitable exoplanets were being found amongst the stars on a regular basis. I am aware of my duties, as I have been for years, but wonder if I may ask if there are details I should know about this case?*

*I have interviewed the suspect who claimed to be a telepathic emanation from a huge alien creature resembling an eyeball the size of a 21st century refrigerator. This man stood up and turned away from me in the midst of conversation, raised his hand to his brow as if in sudden recollection or awareness then disappeared from a locked room. He began to fold at odd angles, turn corners I couldn't see and left in a manner I still don't understand.*

*SSgt F. Chandrastakar*
*Division of Forensic Studies*